KNIGHT
AFTER
KNIGHT

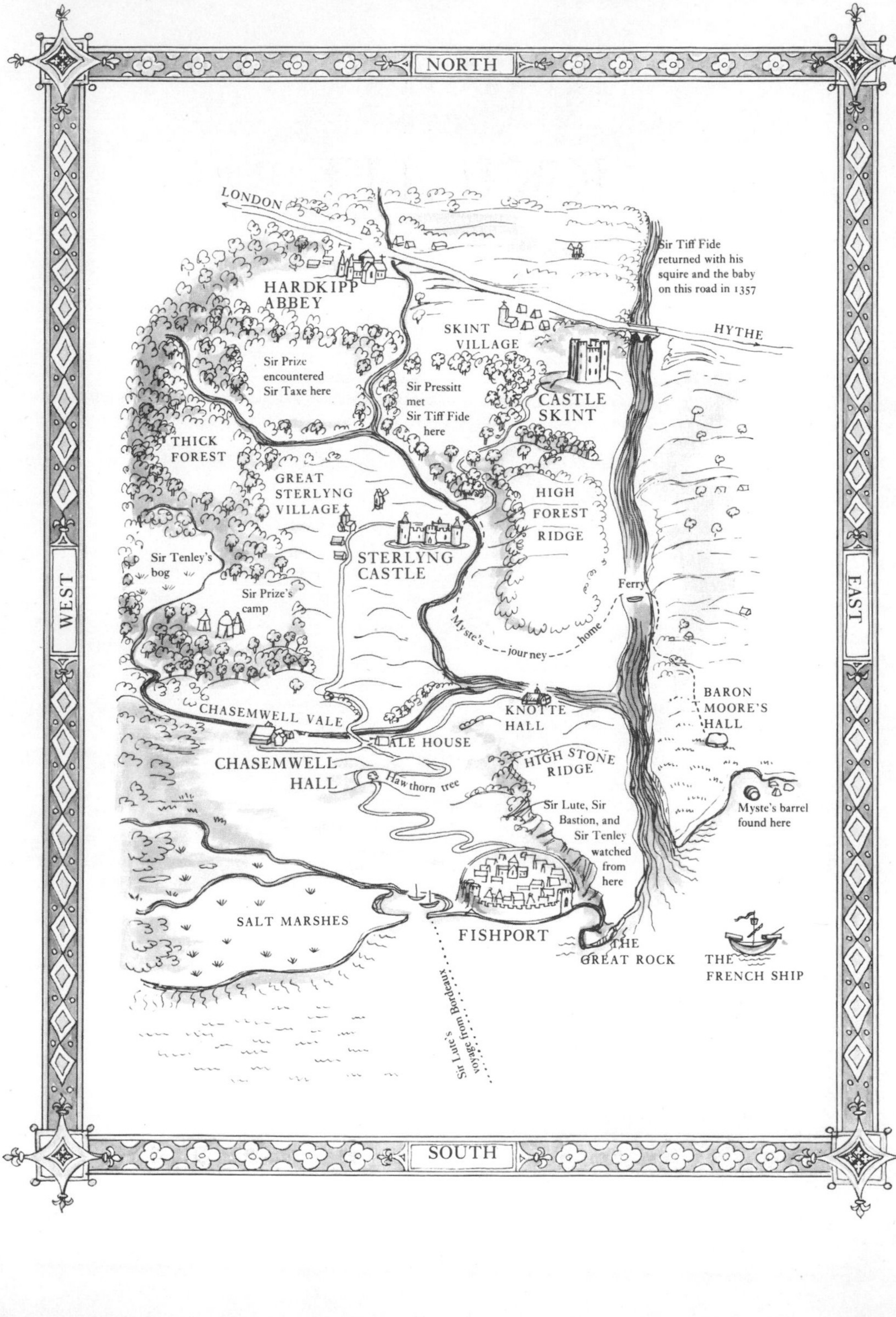

NORTH

WEST

EAST

SOUTH

LONDON

HARDKIPP
ABBEY

Sir Tiff Fide
returned with his
squire and the baby
on this road in 1357

HYTHE

SKINT
VILLAGE

Sir Prize
encountered
Sir Taxe here

Sir Pressitt
met
Sir Tiff Fide
here

CASTLE
SKINT

THICK
FOREST

GREAT
STERLYNG
VILLAGE

HIGH
FOREST
RIDGE

Sir Tenley's
bog

STERLYNG
CASTLE

Sir Prize's
camp

Myste's — journey — home

Ferry

BARON
MOORE'S
HALL

CHASEMWELL VALE

KNOTTE
HALL

ALE HOUSE

CHASEMWELL
HALL

Hawthorn tree

HIGH STONE
RIDGE

Sir Lute, Sir
Bastion, and
Sir Tenley
watched
from
here

Myste's barrel
found here

SALT MARSHES

FISHPORT

THE
GREAT ROCK

THE
FRENCH SHIP

Sir Lute's
voyage from Bordeaux

KNIGHT
AFTER
KNIGHT

Written and illustrated by

SHEILA SANCHA

COLLINS ST JAMES'S PLACE LONDON

William Collins Sons & Co Ltd
London · Glasgow · Sydney · Auckland
Toronto · Johannesburg

First published 1974
© Sheila Sancha 1974
ISBN 0 00 184404 0
Made and Printed in Great Britain by
William Collins Sons & Co Ltd Glasgow

CONTENTS

AUTHOR'S NOTE

Having read the usual standard history books I found the writings of contemporary authors brought the subject to life. Apart from Chaucer's *Canterbury Tales* and *Troilus and Cresside*, my favourite books were the *Froissart Chronicles, Piers the Ploughman, Sir Gawain and the Green Knight* and *The Mabinogion*.

A great deal of research and background reading was necessary for this book and I referred continually to illuminated manuscripts, statues, effigies and brasses for the clothes and armour. My reconstructions of the war machines are based on manuscripts, the work of Sir Ralph Payne-Gallwey and the writings and drawings of Viollet-Le-Duc. The books I found most useful were:

LIFE AND WORK OF THE PEOPLE OF ENGLAND
  Dorothy Hartley and Margaret Elliot (Batsford)
ENGLISH WAYFARING LIFE IN THE MIDDLE AGES J. J. Jusserand
  (T. Fisher Unwin)
CHIVALRY Léon Gautier, trans. by D. C. Dunning (Phoenix House)
THE AGE OF PLANTAGENET AND VALOIS Kenneth Fowler
  (Elek Books)
AN INTRODUCTION TO ENGLISH MEDIAEVAL ARCHITECTURE
  Hugh Braun (Faber)
A HISTORY OF ARCHITECTURE ON THE COMPARATIVE METHOD
  Sir Banister Fletcher (Batsford)
THE CASTLES OF GREAT BRITAIN Sidney Toy (Heinemann)
THE ENGLISH MEDIAEVAL HOUSE Margaret Wood (Phoenix House)
TIMBER BUILDING IN ENGLAND Fred H. Crossley (Batsford)
THE EVOLUTION OF FASHION Margot Hamilton Hill and
  Peter A. Bucknell (Batsford)
ARMS AND ARMOUR Vesey Norman (Weidenfeld & Nicolson)
EUROPEAN ARMOUR Claude Blair (Batsford)
PROJECTILE-THROWING ENGINES OF THE ANCIENTS
  Sir Ralph Payne-Gallwey

Although heavily disguised, Sterlyng Castle is really Bodiam Castle; Castle Skint is Rochester Castle; and Chasemwell Hall is Old Soar Manor House. Fishport is a mixture of Rye and Winchelsea, which was frequently raided at that time.

For advice on the research, I should like to thank Brian Davison of the Department of the Environment, Vesey Norman of the Wallace Collection, Claude Blair of the Victoria and Albert Museum and Margot Hamilton Hill. Also, grateful thanks to John Ryan for volunteering to write out the chapter headings.

*"Certes thai war men and wimen as we er
and ete and drank and logh."*

RICHARD ROLLE OF HAMPOLE *c* 1300

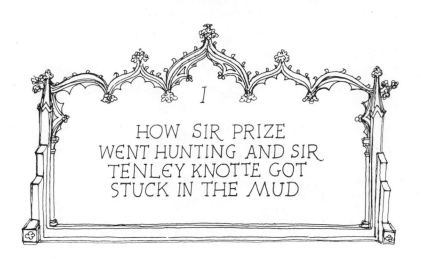

I

HOW SIR PRIZE WENT HUNTING AND SIR TENLEY KNOTTE GOT STUCK IN THE MUD

It was a late afternoon in September, 1372, and long dark shadows were starting to creep over a glowing countryside. There had been a violent thunderstorm the night before, leaving bright puddles in the rough earth tracks, and every leaf had been washed clean. The air was sparklingly clear except where a ghost of a mist hung over the river and clung to a moat enclosing a rectangular area of land, bordered by a stout palisade of split tree trunks. This double defence of wood and water protected Chasemwell Hall, home of Sir Prize.

Chasemwell Hall, a huge barn-like structure, had been built many centuries before by one of Sir Prize's ancestors, an important Saxon thegn. Succeeding members of his family had left their mark; replacing rotten timbers with the new rounded shapes introduced by the Normans and patching it up with wattle and daub. Then Sir Prize's great grandfather – who liked his comforts – had built some private apartments at the north gable end: a great chamber, a chapel and a privy; all at second floor level, with dark store rooms underneath.

Sir Prize had never attempted to repair or alter his homestead. He said that hunting was the only occupation

worth bothering about, and made sure that he never had to do anything else. He was just setting off on yet another hunting party, trotting over the wooden drawbridge and taking the well-worn track across the river and up the hill to the forest beyond; followed by four companions, a few shabby servants, a mixed pack of dogs, and a cart loaded with cooking pots, tents and provisions.

It was always easy to recognize Sir Prize, even from a distance, because of his large red hat – a fold of it flopping in front of his left eye. The hat covered a bald head, but he had a long grey beard to make up for it. His horse, companion of countless hunts, was sturdy, reliable and old. The end of its tail was tied in a knot which flipped to and fro among the flies which, driven away by the storm, had started to return in clouds.

The track widened after they had crossed the river, so Sir Prize invited two of his companions to ride alongside him. One was a friend of long standing, almost as stuffy and boring as himself, called Sir Cum Stance; while the other was a complete stranger, Sir Lute.

Without asking his guests if they wanted to hear it, Sir

2

Prize launched into one of his longest hunting stories; interrupting himself with loud whoops and cries to his dogs.

"Cy va, cy va . . . now where was I? Ah yes, in a distant part of the forest, hounds hot on the scent of wild boar . . . Hoo arere . . . cornered the old devil under a great bank of briar . . ."

The two companions half listened politely. Sir Cum Stance had heard the story so often, he knew it by heart, and was remembering every detail of the last sheriff's banquet; while Sir Lute told himself that he had been abroad so long, he had forgotten how green England was.

Sir Lute was the sort of knight who looked like a knight even when he was wearing only his shirt. There was a strange nobility about him that made people nudge each other and whisper, "Tell me, who is that?"

One of Sir Lute's servants had banged on the great door of Chasemwell Hall, when the thunder and lightning was at its worst the night before, saying that his master, recently landed from Bordeaux, had lost the London road in the storm, and begged shelter for himself and his men. Sir Prize peering through the torrential rain, caught sight of a group of steaming pack horses and a tall black charger, ordered them to be stabled and invited the traveller to come and warm himself and his servants at his smoky old-fashioned fire. Sir Lute had dismounted and walked through the doorway, leaving a trail of muddy footprints on the earth floor; but Sir Prize was vaguely aware that he was entertaining a man of distinction. Visitors from abroad were rare at Chasemwell Hall, and having acquired this one, Sir Prize was loth to let him go again, so had invited him to stay and join him in a few days' hunting. Having reluctantly agreed, Sir Lute was now starting to regret it.

Sir Prize droned on, his beard wagging up and down, and pronouncing the word "boar" with monotonous regularity. The two younger members of the party – both aged about twenty – were careful to keep out of earshot and trotted some way behind. Close friends, they always had plenty to say to each other. One was Sir Prize's only son, Sir Bastion; and the other was the owner of a splendid horse, a horse worth watching.

The owner of this horse was indignant about something Sir Bastion had said.

"Certainly not," said Sir Tenley Knotte – for that was his name. "He's not in the least difficult to control."

"I only wondered . . ." murmured Sir Bastion. "But I like a horse I can rely on."

"Oh, I can rely on this one all right," declared Sir Tenley, keeping an anxious hold on the rein.

Sir Tenley had a long face, long turned-up nose, long chin and long stringy hair. Everything about him was elongated. To make up for the natural misfortune of his features, he dressed with the greatest care and expense. The latest fashion for noblemen was to have the toes of their shoes in long points stuffed with wool. Sir Tenley's shoes were the longest in the district.

On the other hand, Sir Bastion was careless of his appearance. He wore the same clothes year after year, bought new shoes when his feet came through the old ones, and cut his own hair himself with a pair of shears. Everyone liked him and called him a nice boy – which he was.

Sir Tenley's horse, which had been trotting in a restrained but springy fashion, now started indulging in a curious sideways movement. When the rider had got accustomed to this, he started to talk again. "His name is Passemall."

"That's a strange name for a horse."

"Well, I started off by calling him Parzifal – after the hero, you know; but when I'd ridden him once or twice and seen what a fantastic turn of speed he's got, I altered it to Pass-em-all."

4

Sir Bastion looked at the horse doubtfully, then trotted forward to hear if the story was finished, but it wasn't. Sir Prize was only half way through.

". . . with a fierce grunting and squealing, out rushed yet another boar: the biggest, most vicious beast I've ever clapped eyes on . . . Hoo there. Silly white bitch always lags behind . . ."

"Why can't he stop talking and listen to someone else for a change?" complained Sir Bastion, quickly reining back.

"I'd rather hear what Sir Lute has to say," agreed Sir Tenley.

The night before, after Sir Prize had gone to bed, Sir Bastion and Sir Tenley had eagerly questioned the traveller and discovered that he had fought at Poitiers, lived in Aquitaine, been on a crusade with Pierre de Lusignan and witnessed the fall of Alexandria. He had met Pedro the Cruel and crossed the Pyrenees. All this, and Sir Prize was telling him how to kill a boar!

By this time open country had been left behind and they were trotting under the dark trees of the forest: giant oaks reaching up to a tangle of branches overhead, while

5

hawthorn and holly grew thickly underneath. The sun filtered through gaps in the leaves, laying patterns all over the rough earth track and warming the flies that were buzzing round Sir Prize's head more thickly than ever; a crane-fly drifted among them.

Sir Prize had got to the exciting part of his story. "I dismounted, grasped my spear with both hands and looked the great boar unflinchingly in its wicked red eye. The old devil lowered his tusks . . . I braced myself . . ." Sir Prize paused, looked round to see if Sir Bastion and Sir Tenley were listening, opened his mouth and inhaled deeply. The crane-fly disappeared. With a look of astonishment, the speaker closed his mouth and gulped. His bushy eyebrows shot up to an angle of pained inquiry and then dropped to an expression of utter disgust.

That was how the story ended. For the rest of the journey, Sir Prize took care how he opened his mouth and kept his conversation down to tight-lipped monosyllables. Sir Cum Stance politely questioned Sir Lute, asking about some of the foreign countries he had visited; while Sir Bastion and Sir Tenley – a little unsteady on his prancing steed – trotted close behind and listened with interest.

It was nearly dark by the time they had reached the clearing where Sir Prize habitually camped. The five men dismounted, the horses were tethered, the cart unloaded, and the cook and his scullion set to work on the evening meal. Tents were pitched on the fresh green grass. Everyone prepared to spend the night in the forest.

When Sir Prize woke up the following morning in his red striped tent, he looked through the open flap and saw a white pool of mist covering the ground. He could hear someone walking about, collecting sticks for the fire. Soon the smell of trodden grass was mingled with the strong

6

scent of wood smoke. The birds were shouting their heads
off and the sun had started to climb up the sky like an
enormous orange. It was going to be a perfect day.

The mist slowly evaporated as they ate their breakfast
of barley bread and thick home-brewed ale; it was half
gone as they mounted their horses and trotted away; by
the time the sun had soaked it up altogether, everyone
realized that Sir Tenley was living dangerously.

"Someone's given Passemall too much corn," he
complained as he suddenly shot past Sir Prize.

"Can't you learn to keep that animal back, what?" Sir

7

Prize, as master of the hunt, expected to be in the lead.

"Does his horse always go sideways?" inquired Sir Lute, much amused.

"He's got no control over his steed!" exclaimed Sir Cum Stance crossly.

Sir Prize regarded Sir Tenley's antics with profound distaste. Taking a deep breath, he raised his horn to his lips and with the grace of a true huntsman blew a long and powerful blast. The sound rang through the forest and Passemall shot into the distance with the speed of an arrow.

"That's got rid of him," said Sir Prize, giving a longer and even louder blast.

The crashing of undergrowth and drum of galloping hooves died away. There was complete silence.

"Better without him," was Sir Prize's comment.

"Help," cried a distant voice, "Saints have mercy . . . get me out of this."

"I think he's in real trouble," said Sir Lute.

The voice came louder, more urgent. "Blessed Saint Guthlac . . . hermit of the Crowland swamps . . . you've always been good to me . . . saved me when I've been in trouble before. Don't abandon me now . . . For God's sake, don't let me down."

Sir Tenley's desperate appeal to his patron saint ended in a horrible choking sound. Without hesitation, Sir Bastion and Sir Lute spurred their horses forward and disappeared along the track in the direction of the call.

Sir Prize was intensely annoyed. He had been looking forward to showing Sir Lute a thoroughly well-mannered day's sport; and now it was spoilt.

"Devil take that damn fellah and his horse," he said.

"I'd better go and see what's happened," said Sir Cum Stance stiffly.

He trotted towards a pine-covered hill, from the top of which he was able to look down on a stream that wound sluggishly through a large area of thick, black, stinking mud. Mid-stream, floundering and sinking, were the rider and his horse. Sir Lute was on his feet, cutting down small saplings with his hunting knife, while Sir Bastion, also dismounted, was quickly laying them in the mud to form a ramp. Sir Cum Stance trotted back to report to Sir Prize.

"He's fallen into a bog."

"Stupid ass," was Sir Prize's only comment. "That'll give his fine clothes a wash. Come along, we're wasting valuable time."

"You're not going to leave him there?"

"I'm not going to waste a fine morning like this messing about in the mud, if that's what you mean. It's his own fault, what? Anyone could have told him that horse was unreliable. Any case, Bastion and that Lute fellah'll get

9

him out. Come. It's a promising day; we must make the most of the scent while it lies on the ground."

"I prefer to stay," said Sir Cum Stance, disapprovingly.

"By all means. Enjoy yourself rescuing that booby. For myself, I'll continue alone. Unleash the greyhounds," he called to his kennelmen. His temper was rising: if he was to hunt alone, then he would do it properly. He would hunt completely alone. He would leave his servants, he would leave everybody. Calling up his hounds, he continued on through the forest, sitting bolt upright on his ancient horse, not deigning to look back.

II

HOW SIR PRIZE HUNTED ALONE - FOUND TWO STAGS AND LOST HIS TEMPER

Sir Prize did not have a good day.

Having deserted his friends, he jogged along, feeling mean and guilty. He knew he should have stayed and helped to pull Sir Tenley out of the bog; but he wanted to go hunting, he had been looking forward to going hunting, and he did not want to disappoint himself. It was quite obvious that Sir Cum Stance did not think much of his behaviour. The only way to recover his self-respect would be to bring back – single handed – the largest stag that anyone had ever seen. Then they would all be sorry that they had missed such an exciting hunt.

"Ho moy, ho moy, hole, hole, hole," cried Sir Prize, setting his tracking hounds to scent up the game.

It was just the right day for hunting, but the stag Sir Prize was dreaming about didn't seem to be there. He searched the ground, reading the mud and finding traces of hares and rabbits; foxes and badgers; but he was scornful of these. There were no fresh hoof marks leading to the secret hiding place of a stag. By noon the hounds were disheartened and Sir Prize's bad temper was climbing slowly from his boots up to his head via his stomach. He had forgotten to bring any food or drink with him and he blamed the whole situation on Sir Tenley.

"Damn fellah and his cursed horse," he kept on muttering.

Finally the hounds picked up the scent of deer, silently tracing it through the undergrowth. Sir Prize trotted after, his head down, following a steady line of tracks; then he halted his horse and looked about him. Some distance away, under a hawthorn bush, two dry sticks were twitching nervously. It was the stag, trying to flatten itself against the ground, but the tips of its antlers still showed above the fern.

"Cy va, cy va, cy va," cried Sir Prize, loudly summoning up several pairs of hounds who were specially trained to frighten the stag from its bed and set it running. At the second blast from the horn the stag leapt up and started bounding away, followed by all the hounds together in a deep baying chorus.

Sir Prize thundered along behind. His spirits soared: this was the sport he loved. He forced his horse through the thick scrub of the oak woods; galloped rapidly in and out among the beech trees, snapping twigs that lay rotting on the forest floor. He crashed through great tangled thickets of prickly briars, and ploughed a deep trail of flattened nettles and broken bracken in the undergrowth. He spurred his horse up steep hills and hurtled down into valleys, jumping the streams at the bottom and up again the other side, following his hounds closely and crying "Chevauchez, chevauchez," as he went.

He had just reached the top of one of the hills when he saw the stag bounding across a wide grassy space below, chased by two of his best running hounds, and disappearing

into a clump of hazel bushes on the other side. It was a disappointing kind of stag, rather small, but better than nothing. With a loud triumphant, "Holloa," Sir Prize slithered his horse down the bank towards the clearing. Nearly at the bottom, he dismounted, wound up his cross-bow, and fitted a bolt in readiness, expecting the hounds to corner the stag and bring it to bay any minute. Instead, to his utter disgust, the hounds returned, puzzled and nosing round invisible tracks in the grass.

"Devil take those stupid hounds, they've lost the scent," Sir Prize muttered to his horse.

He scanned the bushes for a sign of the stag. To the right of the clearing something moved through the saplings, waving them about. Yes, he could distinctly see the spreading antlers rapidly advancing through the leaves.

"Hou, my friend, hou! He's doubled back!" yelled the hunter, raising the cross-bow.

The stag bounded out. The hounds attacked. The bolt flew through the air. The stag was dead. It all happened in a moment.

Sir Prize looked at the fallen animal with a great deal of satisfaction – then he took a closer look. It was a different, larger stag, with a full fourteen points to its antlers.

Not only was it a different stag, but it was being hunted by a different pack of hounds. They burst into the clearing, and when they saw Sir Prize's pack round their quarry, they attacked whole-heartedly. The air was suddenly filled with a hideous outcry and flying tufts of hair as the dogs, snarling with rage, took each other by the throat and rolled over and over; locked together and howling and screaming between clenched teeth.

Fixing his eyes on the stag, Sir Prize fought his way into

13

the middle of the battle. "Let me go, what? Devil's own cur!" he yelled, trying to shake off a huge mastiff that had fastened itself to his arm. Kicking another dog out of the way, he felt for the stag's antlers, found them, took a firm grip and dragged the dead beast clear of the hounds and over to his horse. He was about to haul it up to the saddle when seven or eight animals in a tight struggling bundle, hurtled past, knocking him off his feet. Sitting on the grass, clutching his hat, he looked for the stag and found it lying in a sinister shadow that hadn't been there before. Sir Prize moved his uneasy eyes round the edge of the shadow until they came to horse's hooves, horse's legs, a boot, the bottom of an expensively-furred gown, and creeping reluctantly upwards finally came to rest on the outraged and purple face of his rich neighbour, Sir Taxe.

For a moment no one said anything. Sir Taxe was so overcome with fury, he was unable to speak. When he finally recovered his voice, the words came bursting out in a splutter.

"Ha. Caught you in the dastardly act, didn't I? Hoped you could get away with it? You enjoy boasting of your prowess with all those tedious stories of yours, then behave quite differently. You don't hunt like a nobleman, Sir Prize, you hunt like a thief."

"Got hold of the wrong idea, Sir Taxe – what? There's been a mistake."

"My eyes don't make mistakes; and they saw you deliberately putting that stag – which is mine – on to that horse – which is yours."

". . . only dragging it clear of the hounds," Sir Prize mumbled guiltily. Both packs were quieter now and only exchanged occasional snarls.

"Liar."

"You've insulted me, using that word, dammit. I won't be called 'liar' in public and take it sitting down."

Sir Prize got to his feet and straightened his back; then he stared hard at the group of splendid noblemen who had now gathered in the clearing. He thought of his own modest party of friends and wished he'd never left them. The bad temper that had been simmering in his stomach earlier in the day now shot to his head and boiled over.

"Who d'you think you are, anyway – what? Such a devilish rich fellah, I suppose, that you feel free to sneer at me – Sir Prize. I wouldn't take 'liar' from the king's mouth, let alone a wool merchant – an upstart."

"Upstart!"

"I'll say it again. Upstart. My ancestors were lords of Chasemwell Vale at a time when yours were digging up the Welsh mud."

Sir Prize swung on his heel and stumbled on a tuft of grass. Glancing to the left, he caught sight of a group of women riding through the trees, a horse litter swaying behind. Sir Taxe must have given the ladies of his household permission to watch the hunt; the litter belonged to his tyrannical old mother, Lady Crippling Taxe, and Sir Prize had a particular horror of her. He wanted to get away before the old witch arrived. Leaving the stag on the ground, Sir Prize stalked across to his waiting horse and climbed into the saddle. Sitting bolt upright, he jogged his

15

steed under a low branch and knocked off his red hat.

"Thief!" shouted Sir Taxe.

"Low-born scurvy villain."

"You're a churl, Sir, a churl."

Sir Prize swung his horse about, the sun shining brightly on his bald head; but the litter was now lurching into the clearing, so he quickly turned to withdraw. Then he got another shock: his own hunting companions had arrived behind his back and stood aghast at the words he had spoken. For his part, he was equally ashamed of *them*. Sir Bastion (his pride, his only son), Sir Cum Stance (usually so presentable), and Sir Lute (the distinguished stranger) all three looked as if they had been deliberately rolling in the mud, just to spite him. The object decorated here and there with old decaying leaves and looking like a well-kept compost heap could only be Sir Tenley Knotte. From his battered hat to the dripping points of his long-toed shoes, he was covered by a thick layer of stinking black-and-green slime. His horse was so weighed down by its mud-clotted mane, it could hardly hold up its head. It was staggering and shaking on its legs. The experience in the bog had nearly been its last.

Sir Prize glared at his party with a concentrated look of accusing fury. Sir Tenley tried a smile, gave it up, then raised his hat in a nervous sign of greeting.

"They managed to get me out," he said.

Sir Prize felt as if he was stuck in the middle of a nightmare and couldn't wake up. He gave his friends a final glower, reversed the direction of his bewildered horse for the third time and confronted his enemies. "Ladies are out of place at a stag hunt," he muttered, fixing his eyes on Lady Super Taxe, Sir Taxe's elegant wife. She edged her palfrey alongside that of her very best friend, Lady Ida Dora Mann and gave her an amused little smirk. Although these women were beautifully dressed, they didn't impress

Sir Prize. He was not happy to see them.

The litter had now come to a standstill, with old Lady Crippling sitting in the front like a painted skeleton. She was not alone; someone sat half-hidden behind her. With a surge of relief, Sir Prize recognized poor Myste, Sir Taxe's ward. She at least didn't matter.

On the other hand Sir Taxe was starting to enjoy himself. His opponent was at his mercy and he always liked a large audience. He greeted Sir Prize's muddy party, put up his hand for silence and addressed the company as if it was a public meeting.

"What is your opinion concerning this man who makes himself out to be such a noble knight – descended, by the way, from such an ancient noble family? Is there anything noble about shooting a stag that's been hunted by another man's hounds? Is there anything noble about driving off the other hounds and trying to keep the stag for himself?"

Everyone agreed that this behaviour was not noble at all. Sir Bastion glanced at Sir Lute and saw him looking very grave.

Sir Prize desperately searched his mind for a way to retrieve his lost dignity. On a sudden impulse, he set his

17

horse in motion, halted before Sir Taxe and slowly pulled off his old hunting gauntlet.

"I won't stand for this, d'ye hear? In this place, before God and these witnesses, I challenge you to mortal combat. Here – I throw down my gage."

Sir Prize flung down the gauntlet which landed on a tall thistle and hung there, gently swaying. Everyone stared at the object that made the quarrel binding. It was an historic moment.

The smile disappeared from Sir Taxe's face. This was something he neither expected nor desired. The last time he had fought – without success – was a good ten years ago, and he did not want to repeat the experience.

The audience turned expectantly from Sir Prize to Sir Taxe. He had no alternative.

"Mortal combat it shall be," he said miserably, reaching down from the saddle and picking up the gage.

There was a sudden burst of conversation.

"Are they going to fight at once – here in the forest?"

"They can't do that – they're not armed."

Everyone wanted to know when and where the combat would take place.

"My father has never behaved like this before," Sir Bastion said to Sir Lute, "I'm amazed, and I'm sure he must have made a mistake."

Sir Lute was not listening. He sat with his mouth open, staring at Lady Crippling's horse litter as if there was a ghost inside it. He seemed completely spell-bound.

"Between me and God, who's the young girl sitting behind the old dame?" he asked.

"She's called Myste." Sir Bastion was rather surprised. "Sir Taxe found her abandoned by the roadside when she was a baby. He's behaved most charitably towards her; brought her up to wait on his mother and calls her his ward."

18

Sir Lute's thoughts were flooded by a surge of vivid memories from the past. "She's strangely like someone I used to know," he said aloud.

Having issued the challenge, Sir Prize sat and thought about it, while his old friend Sir Cum Stance decided to offer his support by making all the arrangements. He was in his element and knew exactly how to behave. He rode across to Sir Taxe and asked him who would act as his second, and Sir Taxe waved the gauntlet he still held in his hand vaguely in the direction of a large man with a grey stubbly chin. This was Sir Charge, who commanded the mercenary troops at Sterlyng Castle, the splendid place where Sir Taxe lived.

"I suggest that the combat is held a week and a day from to-day," Sir Cum Stance started off officiously.

"I see nothing wrong in that," said Sir Charge, who was equally pleased.

"Let's hold a tournament," cried Sir Tenley, forgetting all about the disaster of the bog in his excitement. "Then we can all fight."

Sir Cum Stance gave him a crushing look. "Tournaments are frivolous affairs. You don't settle a quarrel like this at a tournament."

"If you ask my opinion," said Sir Lute, "this is just a

19

simple case of slander and could easily be settled in the courts."

This suggestion did not go down well.

"God's a better judge than man," said Sir Cum Stance stiffly. "There were no witnesses and He knows the rights and wrongs of the affair."

"There's no better way of getting at the truth of an argument than battling it out in armed combat," agreed Sir Charge.

"Then – as they must fight – they should choose a secluded place, a few close friends, and a judge who's reliable and respected by both parties."

"The sheriff will have to be the judge," said Sir Cum Stance. "He would be offended if we asked anybody else."

"Sterlyng Castle has a good jousting field and the lists are still in place – so is the judge's stand," suggested Sir Charge, rubbing his grey chin.

By rights, Sir Cum Stance should have objected to this idea on the grounds that Sterlyng Castle was one of Sir Taxe's many residences; but he loved ceremonious occasions and didn't get enough of them. He didn't want this exciting armed combat to end up as a shoddy little battle hidden away in some glade, as Sir Lute had suggested. Sterlyng Castle was an ideal setting for the sort of armed combat he had in mind.

Everyone carefully listened to the arrangements, determined to watch the fight – private or otherwise.

Sir Prize rode slowly away through the beech trees without even saying goodbye. His temper had fallen back into his boots and taken all his fierce spirit with it. Sir Prize had spent his boyhood learning how to hunt – not to fight. He had never jousted before in his life and had not the faintest idea how to set about it.

Sir Taxe was in a similar state of panic. Cold shivers ran up and down his spine every time he heard the words

20

"armed combat" mentioned, and the person using them most of all was his own wife. She was being quite merry about the quarrel as she discussed it with Lady Ida Dora Mann; while both of them curiously examined the muddy group of horsemen who had appeared so unexpectedly.

"Tell me," whispered Lady Ida Dora, glancing coyly in the direction of Sir Lute, "Who is that?"

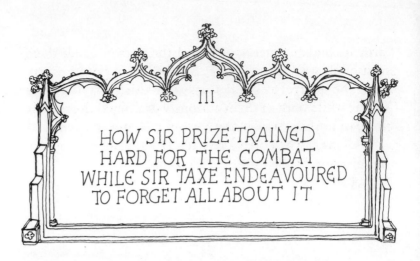

III

HOW SIR PRIZE TRAINED
HARD FOR THE COMBAT
WHILE SIR TAXE ENDEAVOURED
TO FORGET ALL ABOUT IT

Neither Sir Prize nor Sir Taxe felt that eight days were long enough to prepare themselves for the combat; a year and a day would have been better.

Sir Prize was lucky, because his son Sir Bastion was almost as worried as he was himself. A few words spoken over the breakfast ale in the old timber hall was enough to make it painfully obvious that the old man was a complete beginner and would have to learn right from the start.

"What's to be done, Father?" said Sir Bastion, looking increasingly anxious. "I ought to be able to help but, although I had the usual training when I was a squire, I've never been in a battle or even fought at a tournament. You need a highly-skilled man with plenty of experience to give you lessons in combat."

"Someone like me," suggested Sir Lute, with a glance through the open door at his servants, who stood ready and waiting among the loaded packhorses in the courtyard, expecting him to continue his journey to London. "I have fought a great deal – too much for my liking – and would willingly give you some lessons; that is, if you will allow me to stay at Chasemwell Hall until the combat is safely over."

"Stay as long as you like," said the old man, dipping his

crust of bread into the flat ale and staring at it without hope.
"Glad of your company; but as for teaching me how to
joust – huntin's more my line. Never did care for armed
combat."

Sir Lute's offer of help puzzled Sir Bastion. Sir Prize
had behaved badly ever since his guest had arrived: he had
deserted Sir Tenley when he was sinking into the bog; he
had been caught in the very act of poaching Sir Taxe's
stag; and he had completely lost his temper in the argument
that followed. Despite this humiliating display of un-
knightly qualities, Sir Lute was actually proposing to
support the old man in the quarrel. Sir Bastion looked for
a motive explaining this action and failed to find one.

Sir Prize needed to practice on a quintain, and the
village carpenter set one up in the middle of a level area of

wasteland. It took the form of a stout post driven firmly into the ground and sharpened to a point at the top. A shaped hole in the cross beam fitted snugly over this point, allowing the beam to swivel easily. A shield was fixed to one end of it, and a heavy sack of sand hung from the other.

Meanwhile, Sir Prize had been rummaging in the dark store room under the great chamber. Opening a chest, he brought out bundles of mail-armour that must have belonged to his grandfather; they were roughly a hundred years out of date. Two servants lowered the hauberk over his shoulders; it fell jangling down, almost to his ankles, releasing a thick cloud of rusty dust. The sleeves went on right over his hands, forming bag mittens. There were mail chaussees for his legs; but some of the rings were rusted through, leaving ragged holes. Diving back into the chest, Sir Prize was delighted to fish out a yellowish surcoat that had once been white, displaying a faded scarlet chevron – the device King Richard had given to one of his ancestors in the Third Crusade.

"This surcoat was bleached by the sun a good fifty years before I was born," he announced proudly when he had it on.

There was a mail coif to go over Sir Prize's head and shoulders and finally a great, battered, flat-topped helm. Sir Bastion himself laced it on, then stood back to survey his work. He was horrified: his harmless old father had completely vanished; replaced by a sinister iron monster.

The ancient horse was led out of the stable wearing a quilted covering several sizes too large for it; about the same age as the armour, but even more faded and patched.

"That's a hunting horse under the cloth trapper," objected Sir Lute, "he ought to ride a destrier."

"He hasn't got one," said Sir Bastion.

"I could lend him mine."

Sir Bastion shook his head at the notion of his father

mounted on Sir Lute's magnificent war-horse. "He'll have more confidence with his own animal. He's used to it."

It took three of the stable boys to launch Sir Prize into the saddle; then he rode ponderously over to the practice ground, followed by Sir Lute and Sir Bastion. They stood side by side and watched the warrior urge his steed into a rocking-chair canter and attack the quintain with a blunt lance. The sand bag swung in an easy circle and caught him an efficient and semi-stunning blow on the helm, knocking him sideways in his seat.

"You will have to try a faster pace," shouted Sir Lute.

"Eh? What?" came the muffled voice of Sir Prize, who couldn't hear.

"The only way to make that horse go faster is to use hunting calls," said Sir Bastion, "like this." He cupped his hands and suddenly let out a piercing whoop just as Sir Prize was going in to the attack. Cocking its ears, the ancient horse shot suddenly forward. Unprepared, its rider nearly fell off, missed the wooden shield with his lance and hit it a smacking blow with his chest. The sandbag spun round twice and gave him a couple of hard buffets from behind.

"I don't care for this sport," Sir Prize complained, when he had rejoined his companions in a dazed condition.

"It's a matter of timing," Sir Lute bellowed at the right hand side of the flat-topped helm. "You must go faster."

"That's why I let out the hunting cry," shouted Sir

Bastion from the left.

"I prefer to encourage my steed myself," the voice came hollowly, deep inside the helm.

The next time Sir Prize attacked the quintain, he accompanied himself with a gradual crescendo of blood-curdling cries. It sounded like someone being done to death inside a large cracked bell.

"That should scare Sir Taxe out of his wits," Sir Lute remarked.

"I would like to ask a question, only it sounds rather impertinent." Sir Bastion hesitated, searching for the right words.

"Ask whatever you like; but I won't guarantee an answer."

"You are an important man, with a position at court and heavy responsibilities; whereas my father is just a poor country knight. Why are you supporting him in such an unworthy quarrel?"

"Strange behaviour indeed," said Sir Lute, gravely watching Sir Prize, who had lost the quintain altogether and was plaintively hooting his way round the waste land, trying to find it. "I'll tell you this: I met a riddle in the forest – one that has got to be solved. It's about the girl I saw sitting in the litter behind Lady Crippling. To discover the truth, I must find out more about Sir Taxe and his family, and the combat will give me an excellent opportunity."

"I've never heard of any riddle about Myste. I thought you were more interested in Lady Ida Dora Mann," admitted Sir Bastion.

"Saint Paul preserve me from that!" exclaimed Sir Lute.

Sir Taxe did not have the advantages of a kind son and expert tuition; he was handicapped right from the start because he lived in a household of women. A hard, shrewd,

26

successful man in other respects – farm bailiffs, wool traders, ship owners and the like trembled whenever they came near him – he went all to pieces in his dealings with the other sex and their chatter clouded his ability to think. While Sir Prize was busy charging the quintain, Sir Taxe was sitting in the great chamber of Sterlyng Castle, staring through the open door at the ladies' bower beyond, and every time he caught a glimpse of his wife, she seemed to be wearing a different dress.

"Sir Taxe," cried Lady Super, sweeping up the spare folds of her long gown, tucking them under her elbow and holding them tightly against her waist, "what am I going to wear?" She glided through the doorway towards him in her usual elegant way – stomach first, shoulders well back.

"Wear whatever you like," muttered Sir Taxe.

"I must choose between the new robe with the fur lining and this old sideless gown. The new robe is more expensive, but it would be uncomfortable to wear if the weather is hot; whereas this gown suits the occasion perfectly, being embroidered with your arms and mine. It's important to show the company that my father was an earl."

"What company?" demanded Sir Taxe, suddenly alarmed.

"The company coming to watch you fight."

"I expect no company."

"I assure you, everyone will attend."

"This is a private quarrel between myself and Sir Prize," Sir Taxe declared emphatically.

Lady Super shrugged her thin shoulders and returned to the ladies' bower, followed by Sir Taxe, who wanted to see what the women were up to.

The room was well named. It looked like the nest of an untidy, pampered, oriental bird. The air was thick with the scent of lavender. The roof beams were painted scarlet, and the walls gleamed with hangings of brocaded silk.

27

Every chest stood open and the precious contents had been flung on the beds and scattered all over the floor. Several fine chemises – usually folded and hung on rods against the wall – lay crumpled on the carpet, and the large canopied bed was loaded with furs, jewels, enamelled caskets, silk veils and little dogs.

Lady Super took up the heavy, fur-lined robe and held it against herself.

"Which shall I wear?" she appealed to Lady Ida Dora Mann, who was sitting comfortably on the little truckle bed, while the waiting woman, Molly Coddlem, combed out her thick black hair.

"There's nothing wrong with the gown you have on," drawled Lady Ida Dora, not taking her eyes off her own face, reflected in her polished metal hand mirror.

"I'll let Sir Taxe decide." Lady Super took up a new attitude and waited to be admired.

"Yes," said Sir Taxe, weak in the legs and sitting unexpectedly on one of the tiny lap-dogs, hidden under a cloak.

28

"Yes to what? Which shall I wear?"

"Both," said Sir Taxe.

"And what on my head? The new circlet is very fine; but the old coronet shows my rank."

"Certainly," said Sir Taxe, quite overcome by his new worry: how many people would want to watch the fight?

"My dear, he's not paying the slightest attention," said Lady Ida Dora, whose hair had been neatly braided and was now being covered by something akin to a large cushion. "What do you think of my new head dress?"

"I like the pearls."

Finding the conversation unendurable, Sir Taxe left the ladies' bower and slowly wandered downstairs. He wanted someone to confide in, to confess the awful truth that he did not feel up to the combat. Someone to tell him he should start getting into training and make him get on with it. The only person with a strong enough will to do this was his mother, and he found her in the great hall, dictating recipes to the head cook. Sir Taxe's heart sank. Lady Crippling was so old that the only pleasure left to her was eating; whenever she got talking to that enormous man, it was impossible for anyone else to get a word in edgeways.

"Fill a skillet with red wine and set it on the fire to boil. No, better make it a cauldron; we'll need double the amount on account of the number of guests. Add a good quantity of powdered cinnamon – but not too much, cast sugar thereto . . ."

Sir Taxe opened his mouth to ask what guests they were expecting, then shut it again. He didn't want to know. Turning his back, he stood in the doorway leading to the courtyard, listening to the old lady's voice behind him.

"Smite veal, cut it in pieces and cast it to the wine. Prepare small coffins – or pie crusts, if you like to call them that – and bake with the flesh inside until the coffins be done. Then serve it forth."

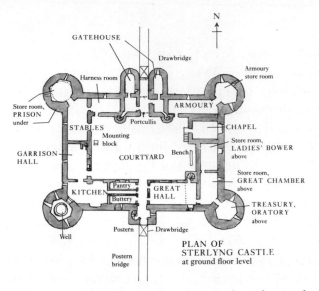

N

GATEHOUSE

Drawbridge

Armoury
store room

Harness room

Store room,
PRISON
under

ARMOURY

STABLES
Portcullis
Mounting
block

CHAPEL

Store room,
LADIES' BOWER
above

GARRISON
HALL

COURTYARD
Bench

Store room,
GREAT CHAMBER
above

Pantry
Buttery

KITCHEN
GREAT
HALL

TREASURY,
ORATORY
above

Well

Postern

Drawbridge

Postern
bridge

PLAN OF
STERLYNG CASTLE
at ground floor level

Sir Taxe stepped into the courtyard and stood there dithering. Any sensible man in his situation would have sent for Sir Charge long ago and arranged to have practice jousts every morning; but Sir Taxe didn't want to get knocked off his horse – repeatedly – by the captain of his own mercenary troops. Least of all under the scornful eyes of his wife.

"The moment they catch sight of me dressed in that ridiculous war harness, they'll forget all about their fine clothes and come running to watch me," he muttered.

A great deal of noise was coming from the armoury opposite, so Sir Taxe walked across and peered round the door. The entire war harness of the castle was being cleaned: mail shirts were being rocked in a barrel of sand to take off the rust; plate armour was being burnished; swords, axes, halberds and daggers were being sharpened. Sir Charge stood in the centre of the room, directing the work.

Sir Taxe shuddered, shut the door quickly and decided to put off practising for the time being. He was still standing irresolute in the courtyard when Myste came hurrying through the gatehouse carrying a basket of herbs

30

she had picked for Lady Crippling from the walled garden beyond the moat. Although she always felt awed and tongue-tied in the presence of her benefactor, she plucked up enough courage to stop and say: "Will it be very dangerous for you my lord, fighting Sir Prize?"

"Dangerous!" blustered Sir Taxe. "I fail to see anything dangerous doing battle with that decrepit old hypocrite. Anyway, I'm in the right, so I can't help but win, can I?"

"I'll be glad when it's over," she said, still looking at him with anxious eyes.

"Stop dawdling girl – you're keeping me waiting," shrieked Lady Crippling, standing in the doorway.

"I'll be glad when it's over too – if I'm still alive to be glad about anything," Sir Taxe muttered, watching her go with a pang of conscience. "Ironic that she should be the one to worry, while all the rest are looking forward to the spectacle of Sir Prize and me murdering each other as if we were just a couple of performing bears."

Sir Taxe listened to the busy noises bombarding him from all sides and then, thoroughly sickened by the whole subject, decided to cast it from his mind and take refuge in the quiet countryside. He walked out of the postern, crossed the rear bridge and came to a large meadow, dotted about with wild daisies, and bordered by the river. It was here that he pastured his finest herd of sheep and he often went to look at them. He had completely forgotten that the double enclosure – so useful at lambing time – had once formed the barriers for the lists; that this was called the jousting field. The sheep had been driven away and he was shocked to find several serfs in their place, busily unloading stakes from a cart and stacking them in neat piles.

The head carpenter was banging the bottom of one of the posts of the enclosure with his boot, shaking his head.

"Them timbers be all perished and rotten," he was saying.

"What's all this about?" demanded Sir Taxe, suddenly wishing he hadn't come.

The carpenter raised his head and Sir Taxe was surprised to see tears in the old man's eyes. "Lord! How this brings to mind your elder brother, Sir Tiff Fide, God rest his soul. A great man for fighting, that he was. Only happy when he was breaking a lance wi' someone."

"Forget about my brother. He's dead," snapped Sir Taxe, furious at the mere mention of his brother's name.

"No offence meant, my lord. But it's nigh on thirty-five year since Sir Tiff Fide last jousted in this field. We mun get them barriers repaired . . ."

"If you don't take those serfs away, I'll have you clapt in irons. They're forbidden to work here," shouted Sir Taxe, red in the face and losing both temper and reason. "Leave the barriers as they are. I'll not have a groat's worth of wood or an hour of a man's time squandered on this field."

"But all be fallen and decayed . . ."

The head carpenter encountered such a powerful glare from his lord that the words died on his lips and he felt as if his whole body had turned to sawdust. Summoning his men, he quickly left the field.

32

Sir Taxe was spoilt and something of a bully. He had been lord of Sterlyng Castle ever since his elder brother had left to fight in France, thirty-five long years before. He did as he liked and he never faced up to anything he didn't like. Confronted by the knotty problem of the armed combat, he looked past it, he looked at it sideways; but he never looked it squarely eye to eye. He got up each morning intending to joust with Sir Charge, but by evening he had put it off.

There was only one place where Sir Taxe was sure of being alone: in his private chapel or oratory. It was a snug six-sided room situated in the turret adjoining his great chamber. It had three windows, a fireplace, a privy and a staircase leading to the roof where he could pace the battlements, enjoying the fresh air. The room was furnished with a reading desk, a book chest containing mainly business accounts, and an altar with a reliquary standing on it, which contained a back tooth of Saint Etheldreda – rather a large tooth for a woman.

For the next two days, Sir Taxe was happy enough, going through his business accounts and leaving his oratory only at meal times and for morning Mass in the castle chapel. Then came Sunday, the Lord's day. Father Off, the chaplain, who had picked up his Latin wherever he could find it, like a sparrow picking up crumbs, and whose prayers must have puzzled the angels, stopped mouthing absurdities and delivered a sermon in plain English which everyone could understand. It was all about the guiding hand of God as he directed the combat from above; making sure that the truthful man should win, and the wrong-doer be shamefully overcome.

"God knows everything," the priest declared, fixing Sir Taxe with his far-away pale blue eyes. "He knows whose conscience is clear as spring water, and whose is foully muddied with hideous sins and wickedness . . ."

It was at this precise moment that a black cloud of doom seemed to settle directly over Sir Taxe's head. It followed him back to his oratory and hovered above, watching him lock the account books back in the chest. He knew that the black cloud of doom was of his own making. It had nothing to do with the quarrel with Sir Prize – he was in the right over that – but what about the shameful secret that gnawed at his conscience and wouldn't leave him alone, even now. God would know all about that. And if God wouldn't protect him – who would? He had done nothing to prepare for the armed combat; he hadn't even tried on his armour. In his panic, he fell flat on his face before the altar and addressed his patron saint in much the same way as he would dictate a letter to an influential friend.

"Gracious Saint Etheldreda. I'll give you a pair of gilt bronze candlesticks, almost three-feet high and finely worked; I know of a place where they can be made. They will stand here on the altar beside your tooth if you will promise to make something happen to stop the fight. Send a flood, an earthquake, a tempest. Make Sir Prize drop dead of a fit; give him the plague; let him be bitten by one of his own dogs. Use whatever means you like – fair or foul – but keep him at home on the day of the combat."

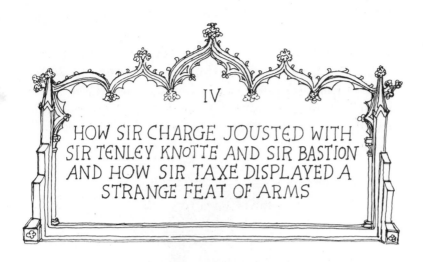

IV

HOW SIR CHARGE JOUSTED WITH SIR TENLEY KNOTTE AND SIR BASTION AND HOW SIR TAXE DISPLAYED A STRANGE FEAT OF ARMS

Saint Etheldreda turned a deaf ear to Sir Taxe's bribe of candlesticks, or perhaps she could not hear through her tooth, for no natural disaster came to spoil the fine autumn weather. Sir Taxe woke up one morning, counted the days and found there was only one left to count. It was Tuesday. Tomorrow, he was in grave danger of being killed by Sir Prize.

Sir Taxe resolved to spend this final day in a desperate attempt to prepare himself for the combat; but when he opened the door of his hall after breakfast and stepped into the courtyard, he found to his horror that Sterlyng Castle was being invaded by all the nobles of the surrounding countryside, together with their ladies. How could he practice with such an audience? Lady Super Taxe, wearing the sideless gown, was behaving like royalty as she glided through the crowd. Lady Ida Dora Mann followed close behind.

"God's vengeance! What are these people doing here?" snorted Sir Taxe, glaring round and hating everyone he saw. "They'll get no welcome from me, so send them away."

"But they're all your friends, come to support you in your quarrel, my lord," replied Lady Super. "I told you

35

they'd be here. They'd be offended if you sent them away."

"That dotard, shuffling through the gatehouse, supported by two worthless yellow-haired squires has the look of Sir Parr Stitt. It *is* Sir Parr Stitt. He's even brought a herald and two trumpeters with him. What's he here for? I didn't invite him."

"It was Sir Charge who made the arrangements. He asked him to judge the combat."

"Sir Charge should have kept his nose out of my business. This is a private quarrel and Sir Prize and I will battle it out on our own. We won't be watched, d'ye hear?"

"You had better stop shouting and remember that Sir Parr Stitt is a man of great importance," hissed Lady Super. "We must greet him properly; he's the sheriff and represents the king."

Sir Taxe sulkily raised his hand. His wife touched it with the very tips of her jewelled fingers, and together they crossed the courtyard in stately fashion.

"God prosper you and welcome to Sterlyng Castle," said Sir Taxe, meaning neither of these things.

"Thought you were dead years ago," mumbled Sir Parr Stitt, peering short-sightedly at the vague shape of his host. "Killed at Poitiers, they told me."

36

"No. That was my elder brother, Sir Tiff Fide."

"Glad you recovered." Sir Parr Stitt, who never heard much of what was said, found it easier not to listen. He turned to Lady Super. "So this is your wife, Lady Cinque Tiff Fide."

"No. That was my brother's wife. She died in the year of the great plague."

"Greetings, Lady Cinque Tiff Fide."

Lady Crippling came stumping down the chapel steps, leaning heavily on her stick. "Who's this?" demanded Sir Parr Stitt, when she floated into his field of vision.

"You remember me!" screamed the old lady, her shrill cracked voice cutting through his deafness like a sharp knife. "We were friends at the court of King Edward – the present King's father – God rest his poor murdered soul."

"That's it," cried Sir Parr Stitt, suddenly coming to life. "Now I know who you are! Devilish fine woman you were then . . . behaved like a devil as well . . ."

Sir Taxe left the old couple conversing in shouts and told his wife she would have to welcome the guests without him. Then he fled back to his oratory and firmly bolted the door.

The invasion of Sterlyng Castle went on all day. Apart from the great nobles riding proudly over the drawbridge on their magnificent horses, the common people had decided to treat the event as a public holiday. They came tramping across the fields, riding along the roads and rowing up the river. On their arrival, they went straight to the jousting field and settled on the ground surrounding the lists. Soon it was difficult to find a spare patch of grass to sit on.

Sir Prize and his party arrived just before dusk, bringing with them a warlike cart loaded with armour and weapons. Sir Taxe watched them through his narrow window as they pitched their tents on the rising ground between the lists and the trees growing at the side of the road. Sir Prize's banner fluttered over a pavilion that was lined with faded scarlet satin, while his shield, carrying the arms of a field divided per chevron argent and gules, hung from the branch of a handy oak. Sir Taxe continued to watch while his enemy ate a hearty supper, and then through the darkness of the evening, he saw his flickering fire. Listening, he caught the soft sound of a popular tune being played on a lute.

"This is no time for feasting and carousing!" exclaimed Sir Taxe, closing the wooden shutter with a bang.

Despite the fact that Sir Prize was tone deaf and only capable of roaring out hunting songs, he found the music comforting. He sat on a faldstool with his head drooping and his long grey beard lying flat against his chest, while the firelight glimmered on his large red hat, turning it orange. He kept his eyes glued to Sir Lute's fingers as they moved rapidly across the strings, amazed that anyone who wasn't a minstrel could play as well as this. When Sir Lute started to sing, Sir Bastion and Sir Tenley Knotte joined in with the choruses.

In the great hall of the castle, Lady Super and Lady Ida Dora sat on either side of the window; they had flung the shutters open and were listening too. Myste was even more attracted by the music. She slipped quietly through the postern and crept to the end of the bridge. She looked like a shadow until a sudden leaping flame from one of the fires lit up her old green dress.

Sir Lute stopped playing and looked intently at her; then carefully plucking the strings with the goose quill, he outlined a sweet lilting tune, as if in her honour. The song, composed by some troubadour of Provence, was a hundred years out of date. "Quant voi la Rose . . ."

The change of melody did not go unremarked in the great hall.

"That is the voice of my next husband," declared Lady Ida Dora. "All my previous husbands have been such decrepit old men that this time I have decided to please myself."

"But you don't know anything about him, or his family," objected Lady Super.

Sir Taxe watched the sunrise on Wednesday morning and wondered if it would be the last time he would see it. He sent a messenger to inquire after the health of Sir Prize, hoping he might have died in the night; but he was reported to be in the best of health and had breakfasted heartily on bread, a piece of salt fish, and half a pottel of ale.

At morning Mass, Sir Taxe ignored Father Off's mumbling prayers and delivered his final ultimatum direct to God, for he had begun to lose faith in Saint Etheldreda. He would give the candlesticks to the village church if he survived the morning unhurt; and he would throw in a gold cross as well, if God, by some miracle, could manage to make him victorious.

The crowd in the jousting field had spent an uncomfortable night. Folk were stiff and sore from lying on the ground, they had been awake a long time, and some of them were hungry. There had been no sign of either Sir Prize or Sir Taxe since daybreak. They had had nothing to watch other than a succession of scullions carrying food over the bridge from the postern gate to a large tent that had been pitched under the trees at the far side of the moat. Trestle tables and benches stood near, so that the barons and their ladies could sit and refresh themselves in the pleasant shade.

40

The sight of so much food made the ragged people hungrier than ever. The more boisterous fellows among them began to quarrel, laying bets on the outcome of the fight.

"Up Sir Prize, Sir Prize and the scarlet chevron," chanted Sir Prize's liege men, provoking all the loyal feelings of Sir Taxe's dependants.

"Up Sir Taxe, Sir Taxe and the golden ram!" responded the other half of the crowd, indulging in fisticuffs.

Sir Prize stood miserably inside his pavilion, dressed in his long mail hauberk and surrounded by the more important members of his party. Sir Lute, who had been giving him last minute instructions, paused to listen to the uproar outside, then left the pavilion to see what was happening.

"It looks as if there's going to be a riot," he remarked to Sir Tenley, who had followed.

"I hope so." Sir Tenley grinned. He had ordered some new armour from Italy many months ago, and it had just arrived. He was longing for an excuse to wear it.

"Look, here comes Sir Taxe," Sir Bastion shouted above a sudden roar of applause. The postern gate was flung open and Sir Taxe came out. He looked like a man who had been condemned to death as he moved unsteadily along the bridge. Behind, in proud procession, came Sir Parr Stitt, Lady Crippling, Father Off, Lady Super, Lady Ida Dora, and many other knights and ladies. The castle garrison of eight bowmen and twenty footmen-at-arms, all wearing Sir Taxe's badge and fully armed, came marching in the rear, led by their sergeant, Hugo First.

Sir Prize showed himself for a moment at the entrance of his pavilion, then retired again inside. He didn't say anything because of the way his teeth were chattering.

Sir Cum Stance, acting as Sir Prize's official representative, drew himself up very straight, and stiffly walked across to parley with the enemy.

"Greetings and good health," he said, addressing Sir Charge, "the barriers are in a bad state of repair."

"Good enough for to-day," said Sir Charge uncomfortably. He had completely forgotten to check them.

"Why hasn't the grass been mown and covered with sand?"

"Conditions are the same for both."

"The crowd seems to be getting out of hand."

Completely ignoring the enthusiastic cheers of his supporters, Sir Taxe stalked over to the pavilion that had been prepared for him and went inside. Old Lady Crippling followed her son to watch him being armed and give him the good advice she should have delivered many days ago.

Meanwhile, the rest of the company paraded to and fro, showing off their splendid clothes. Sir Lute soon discovered that wherever he walked, Lady Ida Dora seemed to be walking beside him. He noticed that her gown was trimmed with the finest ermine; that her fingers were stiff with filigree rings; and that the large jewels flashing on the gold band of her overgown were diamonds and sapphires – a rich woman hunting for a husband. But Sir Lute was not the man to be lured by such extravagant bait.

42

As it happened, they were passing the judge's stand which had been draped with musty silk hangings. Sir Lute looked up and was immediately confronted with the clue he had been searching for: there were two shields embroidered on the canopy; one showing the golden ram of Sir Taxe; the other depicting a strange black animal, half dog, half fish; an animal Sir Lute was well acquainted with.

"Why are the arms of Tiff Fide displayed alongside those of Taxe?" he asked casually.

Lady Ida Dora gave her companion an arch sideways glance and wondered if, after all, her new head dress was the wrong shape to suit her, he seemed so utterly unimpressed.

"Sir Tiff Fide was Sir Taxe's elder brother," she explained. "He kept the ancient Welsh name because he was proud of it; whereas Sir Taxe prefers the title and arms given to his grandfather when he abandoned Llewelyn and joined King Edward's forces in 1282."

Having acted on a vague hunch and discovered evidence to prove it right, Sir Lute quickly gave Lady Ida Dora the slip and went in search of Myste. He found her walking along the river bank talking to Sir Bastion and looking too happy to be disturbed. Sir Lute told himself that her likeness to her mother was uncanny. It was fascinating just to watch her. A walking ghost. How old was she – about sixteen? Yes. Her mother had been dead for exactly sixteen years. So, Sir Taxe was lying when he called her a foundling. But what had become of Sir Tiff Fide?

By now, the sun had reached its height, and ragged bullies were elbowing their way through the noisy crowd into the best positions. There was an awed hush as Sir Prize, wearing his faded surcoat and carrying the flat-topped helm, emerged into the open, crossed the grass, and sat himself carefully on a carved wooden chair that

stood waiting for him. He continued to sit there, staring apprehensively at Sir Taxe's pavilion, for an interminable three-quarters of an hour; but there was no sign of the enemy. The sun started to descend and Sir Parr Stitt, who had taken his place in the middle of the stand and was enjoying the company of so many beautiful ladies, began to be uncomfortably aware of the hardness of the bench. The two trumpeters, who had announced Sir Prize's arrival with a loud triumphant flourish, relaxed, lounged against the barriers and started chatting idly with the herald.

There was grave trouble in Sir Taxe's pavilion. He was standing on a small carpet, scarlet in the face from trying to hold himself in, while Sir Charge struggled to do up the straps of a coat of plates – a species of cloth-covered iron corset.

"It's no good," said Sir Charge, releasing the straps and rubbing his grey chin. "They're about an inch too short, and even if they did meet, he would never be able to breathe properly."

"You've let yourself get fat and idle," said Lady

44

Crippling, scornfully surveying her son.

"New straps will have to be fitted," continued Sir Charge. "And then there's the jupon as well." He picked up the richly-embroidered garment that went over the coat of plates. "The seams will have to be unpicked at the sides and laced. The work will take a good two hours."

"The rabble won't wait as long as that," said Lady Crippling, listening to the angry turmoil that had started up again outside. "It's your fault, Sir Charge. It was your responsibility to check the armour, so you'll have to amuse the crowd and keep them quiet while the alterations are being made. Pick a quarrel with someone – anyone – I suggest a knight of Sir Prize's party. Challenge him to a joust."

A look of satisfaction flickered over Sir Charge's grim face. He was a stupid man, but he knew how to fight and welcomed this chance to show off his skill. He immediately left the pavilion, strode towards the stand, and stopped spell-bound with indignation in front of Sir Tenley, who was hopping about on one foot, showing the ladies how to walk in long-toed shoes.

"It must be awkward, going up stairs," Lady Super remarked.

"Oh, I've had to go up stairs backwards ever since getting these shoes."

"What happens if you're in a hurry?" asked Lady Ida Dora.

"Then – by me troth – it's quicker to take them off."

Sir Charge couldn't wait any longer. He brushed the ladies aside and pushed himself forward. "Your shoes are an insult to God and man," he shouted. "The toes are too long."

"No they're not," protested Sir Tenley mildly. "They're in fashion."

"Then your tunic's too short and its sleeves are too wide."

45

Dumb with surprise, Sir Tenley stared down at the hem of his brief tunic and fingered the fine squirrel lining of its voluminous sleeves.

"Is anyone here carrying a pair of shears?" Sir Charge appealed to the mob. "I'll crop your hair. Long hair is degenerate anyway; but long straight hair is disgusting. Why isn't it curled?"

"By me troth," said Sir Tenley, suddenly brightening up. "If you're asking for a fight, then I'm your man. My hair's my own business and I defend my right to keep it so, body for body." A fashionable gauntlet was tucked in his belt. He pulled it out and flung it to the ground.

"Go arm yourself and I will do likewise," said Sir Charge, picking it up.

All this time, Sir Taxe had been sitting in his pavilion, making his confession to his mother.

". . . so I can't fight. I'm out of practice."

The old lady was astonished. "Why, there's nothing to it!" she exclaimed. "It'll be as easy to tumble Sir Prize from his horse as it is to knock a mangy old crow off a wall."

"I couldn't even do that. I haven't held a lance for twenty years."

Lady Crippling thought for a while and then came up with a solution.

"There's one of Sir Tiff Fide's great lances hanging in the hall. It's longer than any lance Sir Prize is likely to have."

"But aren't lances measured before a combat?"

"Yes, but you would take up the great lance *after* the weapons have been checked."

"You're a clever woman Mother," said Sir Taxe admiringly, giving a deep sigh of relief.

Before long, Sir Charge came riding down from the castle wearing a surcoat of green stripes and a brightly-polished helm. His horse was a big-boned, thick-set

Flemish stallion and Passemall seemed half its size by comparison as he pranced out of Sir Prize's camp. Such an unusual light-weight war horse, together with his new armour, made Sir Tenley the immediate favourite of the crowd, who regarded him as knighthood's finest flower. His tight-fitting jupon was embroidered with the Knotte device, there were long toes to his new sabatons, and his helm was of the latest design for the joust; the lower half projecting beyond the sight, which gave him a look of great determination.

Lady Crippling hurried out of her son's pavilion, struggled up the steps of the stand and settled herself heavily on the bench beside Sir Parr Stitt. She didn't intend to miss the fun.

The two contestants entered the lists at opposite ends and proceeded towards the centre: Sir Charge's stallion at a grave slow trot and Passemall with his usual springy sideways motion. The knights met, turned, saluted Sir Parr Stitt and the ladies, gave the herald their names and then returned to their respective ends.

Sir Charge's horse awaited the starting signal with its hooves planted firmly on the ground; whereas Passemall delighted the crowd, entertaining them with a complicated oriental dance.

47

"Sound the trumpets and set forward the combatants," yelled Sir Parr Stitt.

The trumpets blared out loud, clear, and in a terrible discord. Sir Charge couched his lance and urged his horse to a canter; but by the time he had settled himself in the saddle and taken aim, his target was no longer there. Passemall – who hated any sort of unpleasant noise – had flicked back his ears, tucked in his tail, shot past Sir Charge and quitted the lists with his usual fantastic turn of speed.

Now Sir Tenley's new helm had been specially designed for the joust. Leaning forward to attack, the wearer could see reasonably well; but encountering the shock of the enemy, his body was flung back, his eyes automatically protected by the projecting lower part of the helm and visibility was severely restricted. Sir Tenley, leaning back and pulling on the reins of his runaway horse, had a clear view of the sky, but nothing else. If he had been able to see properly, he might have steered Passemall another way.

"What's happened?" Sir Parr Stitt demanded, peering down at the lists.

"He's lost control of his horse," Lady Crippling screamed. "Adam's bones, he's heading straight for the food tent."

Passemall thundered in at one side of the tent and came out the other, a confused tangle of ropes, shreds of canvas, jellied eels, rags of silk, quails, woodcock and plover. Stuffed swans and legs of venison seemed to take wing and fly; while wheatmeal trenchers, sugar plums and all the little coffins that had taken so long to prepare, were rolling away over the grass like surprised rabbits. The hungry crowd roared its delight and ran in the wake of Passemall, picking up as much food as it could lay its hands on. The horse was even more frightened by this new noise, and bolted down the field as if it were running a race. Sir Tenley, thinking a circle was safer than a straight line, pulled hard on the left-hand rein just as he was galloping along the river bank. Passemall did an abrupt turn and leapt into the water.

"Behold the high-stomached, foolish knight," shouted Sir Charge, who had followed, alternately waving to the crowd and pointing a scornful finger at his opponent floundering in the river.

"Shame on me if I let these words pass," cried Sir Bastion, running up, hotly loyal to his friend.

"That knight's a degenerate ninny, you've only got to look at him." Sir Tenley, his armour heavily-waterlogged, was being laboriously dragged from the river by his armpits, while his steed clambered up the bank.

"I defend my right to deny it body for body," yelled Sir Bastion, pulling off his hood and flinging it to the ground in fury.

"Someone pass me up his gage and I'll teach this young jackanapes a lesson," said Sir Charge.

Sir Bastion wouldn't have been quite so quick to defend his friend if Myste hadn't been there, and if he hadn't suddenly fallen under the enchantment of her large dark eyes.

A short time later, Myste was sitting at the back of the stand, nibbling her nails with anxiety. Having admired Sir Bastion ever since she could remember, their morning conversation had given her great happiness. Now everything was to be spoilt. He was going to fight Sir Charge and she didn't want to see him overcome, humiliated and hurt before her very eyes.

The judge was asleep when Sir Bastion and Sir Charge entered the lists, and Lady Crippling had to prod him awake with her stick. "Set forward the combatants," said Sir Parr Stitt hurriedly, before they were properly ready, facing each other at the far end of the lists.

The trumpets sounded and the lances were lowered.

49

The two knights spurred towards each other at full gallop; but Sir Bastion's horse shied away when they should have made the encounter, and the weapons hit nothing. There was a groan from the crowd and Sir Charge became more confident than ever.

Sir Bastion was very angry with himself and his horse. He took a tighter hold on the rein, adjusted the shield laced to his shoulder and directed a careful aim at the far-away figure of Sir Charge, who was doing the same.

Urging his horse to a thundering speed, Sir Bastion crashed his lance against Sir Charge with such a shock that the horses fell back on their haunches and he was nearly forced out of the saddle. He raised his arm and let the broken handle of his splintered lance fall away. His squire was waiting at the far end of the lists to hand him a fresh one.

Before the third course, Sir Bastion remembered all the rude words Sir Charge had used on his friend. He thought of Myste watching. He looked along the lance and bore down on Sir Charge with such cool determination that he smote him well and truly in the centre of the shield, splitting it from top to bottom. He felt the grate of metal against metal as the lance found the plate armour under the striped green surcoat. The heavy knight jerked out of the saddle and landed half his steed's length behind it on the grass.

Now it was Sir Bastion's turn to become the idol of the

crowd. The applause was tumultuous. Myste stopped biting her nails and found herself shouting louder than anyone. Lady Ida Dora leant gracefully over the side of the stand and asked Sir Lute if he had been giving his young friend a little instruction. Sir Lute replied that he hadn't.

By this time, Sir Taxe's squires had finally managed to squeeze him into his armour. The crowd went wild with excitement, hats and hoods were thrown into the air, when he walked out of his pavilion. There was a gap at the side of his jupon, criss-crossed with new laces.

Sir Prize was so stiff from sitting still that he could hardly unbend and rise from the chair of state. "It's taken half the day for you to summon up the courage to face me!" he yelled at his opponent.

Sir Taxe ignored this remark and stumped over to the opposite chair, the plates of his leg armour clinking agreeably.

"You, the appellant," cried the herald, standing forward and addressing Sir Taxe, "in the name of God, say who you are and the nature of your quarrel."

"My quarrel's my own affair and it's none of your business," muttered Sir Taxe, in no humour for this sort of nonsense.

"We'll proceed according to the laws of combat," the herald countered severely.

"I'm known to everyone here, so there's no need to tell them," said Sir Taxe doggedly. "And as for my quarrel with Sir Prize, I caught him stealing my stag, as God is my witness." The herald held out a bible and Sir Taxe laid his hand on the huge silver-gilt, jewel-encrusted cover.

The herald turned his attention to Sir Prize. "You, the defendant. Give your name and your answer."

"Fellah lies in his teeth – what? I am Sir Prize, Lord of Chasemwell Vale, and a better huntsman than the cowardly upstart accusing me. I'm able to catch me own beasts

51

without any help from him – better ones too. I've no interest in his mangy flea-bitten quarry." He then told the whole story about his mistake and swore on his bible oath that it was true.

The champions turned their backs on each other and stalked over to their waiting mounts. Sir Prize was laced into his flat-topped helm, and Sir Bastion helped him mount, while Sir Lute handed up the lance. Then they both wished him luck and promised to pray for success.

The herald took both lances, found them equal in length, and returned them to their owners.

Sir Prize's ancient horse, completely hidden under the cloth housing except for its hooves, nose and watchful eyes, jogged stolidly to the end of the lists. It was a bit put out as two of Sir Taxe's pages started fighting and yelling just beyond the barrier – having been paid to create a diversion. The audience turned to stare at them while Sir Taxe, at the other end of the lists, quietly exchanged his weapon for the great lance of Sir Tiff Fide.

When the disturbance had died down and the two pages been suitably reprimanded, Sir Parr Stitt gave the signal to start.

"Toot, to to toot, to to toot," rang out the trumpets.

"Trour, trour, trourourourour!" hooted Sir Prize, to the immense amusement of the crowd, as his ancient horse moved into action. "Cy va, cy va, cy va," trying to get it to go faster.

Sir Taxe, riding on an enormous mettlesome destrier, was advancing from the other end of the lists and having trouble in couching his lance; it was about twenty feet long and dreadfully heavy. He had tried to lower it slantwise over his horse's neck, but the infuriating creature had flung up its head, causing an obstruction. He trotted along with his lance parallel to his horse on the right side, when it should have been inclined to the left, and the point was dropping down at every jolt.

"Sha hou, swef, my friend, swef," yelled Sir Prize, charging along at a splendid pace.

"Must find a way to smite the old devil," muttered Sir Taxe, altering the line of approach to an unorthodox sideways angle while the destrier started to gallop and his lance dropped another six inches.

"Stupid fellah's not coming at me properly," said Sir Prize, swerving to meet Sir Taxe who, having dropped the reins altogether, was using both hands to try to lift his outsize weapon.

Sir Prize braced himself for the encounter just as the point of Sir Taxe's lance got caught in a tuft of grass. Impelled by the momentum of his horse, he left the saddle and soared through a twenty-foot arc right over his enemy's head.

"Trout, trout, trout," whooped Sir Prize from below, anxiously searching for his opponent and never thinking of looking skywards and spearing him from below.

Sir Taxe made a graceful descent and a very noisy landing; crashing down on the sun-baked earth with a terrifying clatter and thump.

There was a moment's shocked silence, after which the crowded field echoed from end to end with a deafening roar of laughter. People fell into such fits of merriment, they were doubled up, bellowing as if they were ill. The joke was catching; even the fine ladies up in the stand were rocking about, holding their sides and flinging themselves into each other's arms, shrieking with mirth. This movement was altogether too much for the rotten timbers supporting them and the whole structure collapsed sideways and tipped its load – regardless of rank – on to the ground.

"Ooh, ooh, ooh," wailed Lady Super, pulling her veil over her face, and rocking to and fro in a kind of biblical despair.

"Adam's bones, hold your noise, can't you?" remonstrated Lady Crippling who had landed on top of Sir Parr Stitt and was busily disengaging her rings from his beard.

"Help," Lady Ida Dora was calling softly, because only Sir Lute was meant to hear.

He helped her to her feet, inquired if she was hurt, and then hastened away to see what had happened to Myste; but he needn't have bothered. Sir Bastion had already found her.

"Look!" Myste screamed, in great distress. "Sir Prize is going to cut off Sir Taxe's head!"

Sir Prize, who had been wandering round the lists, uttering anxious hoots, waving his lance and searching for his enemy, had finally come across him lying in the grass. Sir Prize had dismounted, unlaced his opponent's helm, found he was not dead, and was wondering what to do next. For want of a better idea, he had begun to draw his sword.

"I can't bear the sight of blood. I swear I shall faint," murmured Lady Ida Dora, swaying gracefully in front of Sir Lute; but he was looking the other way and she had to fall into the arms of the maid, Molly Coddlem.

Sir Lute hurried over to the barrier and started yelling at Sir Prize. "Sheath your sword and drag him from the field."

Sir Prize nodded his head several times to show he had heard, and shoved his weapon back in its sheath. Then he bent down, took hold of Sir Taxe's feet and slowly trundled him out of the lists.

There was no doubt in anyone's mind about who had won the combat.

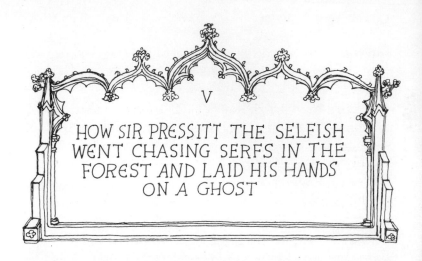

V

HOW SIR PRESSITT THE SELFISH WENT CHASING SERFS IN THE FOREST AND LAID HIS HANDS ON A GHOST

Now there was only one man in the whole countryside who had not gone to watch the armed combat; and that was a bad-tempered bachelor, well on the wrong side of forty, whose name was Sir Pressitt. He hated meeting people, avoided jolly gatherings like merrymaking at Christmas and harvest time; kept carefully away from fairs and feasts; and his gatehouse door was always shut to anyone who happened to knock on it. He was well-known for his poor hospitality. At the very same moment that Sir Prize was trying to hit Sir Taxe with the sharp end of his lance, Sir Pressitt was creeping round his part of the forest on the look-out for runaway serfs.

Ever since the Black Death, some twenty-four years before, there had been a scarcity of men to work on the land. Serfs, who by law were compelled to live all their lives in the same village and work for their feudal lord, had taken to escaping to some other part of the country where a landowner would hire them for wages, asking no questions. It was better still if they could get to a town. Sir Pressitt had lost a lot of good men this way.

"I hear somebody coming," murmured Sir Pressitt, who had developed the habit of talking aloud to himself because

he lived alone. He crawled into the middle of a thick hazel bush to hide and keep watch.

Feet were shuffling through dry leaves. A thin white hand parted the bracken opposite and a ragged, hairy, ghost-like creature came stumbling forward at a fast hobble.

"Ha! Got you!" yelled Sir Pressitt, bursting from his bush and grabbing the apparition by the ear.

"Ho!" gasped the victim of this attack.

"Admit you were escaping and don't try to deny it," continued Sir Pressitt, still gripping the ear. But he wished he had looked harder before he leapt, not being sure if he had caught hold of a man or a spirit, and Sir Pressitt had a horror of the supernatural.

"Unhand me, villain. This is no way to treat a knight," came a croaking voice, while the thing twisted its face round and stared at Sir Pressitt with such weird red-rimmed eyes, they sent shivers shooting up his spine.

"It's I who want to know who you are," he said uncertainly, tweaking the ear by way of experiment, to see if it was real. "What's your name and what village are you from?"

"My name is Sir Tiff Fide the Bold."

Sir Pressitt released the ear as quickly as if it had the plague. "Don't be an idiot," he shouted, jumping behind a tree. "Sir Tiff Fide was killed at Poitiers; everyone knows that."

The apparition tugged anxiously at its wild white hair, then carefully inspected the edge of its gown. It hung in shreds, like a dirty cobweb.

"If I'd lost my life at Poitiers, I'd be dead – which I'm not, as you can see."

Sir Pressitt stared, unconvinced. The face was the unearthly colour of a corpse; but the red nose in the middle of it sniffed reassuringly. If it actually was a ghost, then it had caught a terrible cold. Summoning up every bit of his courage, he put both hands on the skeleton-like shoulders and gave them a good shake. He could almost hear the bones rattling about inside the skin; but there were hard bones.

"Could you really be Sir Tiff Fide?"

"Of course I am," came the hoarse whisper, "why should I lie?" Then he suddenly clutched Sir Pressitt's long sleeve. "Think of it: Sir Tiff Fide the Bold, chained like a dog in a kennel; buried alive for fifteen years beneath the flagstones of his own castle. But now I'm out, I must quickly make good my escape. Rally my friends. Appeal for justice."

The fugitive started to shuffle off, but Sir Pressitt strode behind and put a firm detaining hand on his shoulder.

"Escaped from Sterlyng Castle?"

"Where else?" he cried impatiently, looking wildly back the way he had come, struggling with a grip that got tighter. "Time's short. I must be through the forest and reach the sanctuary of Hardkipp Abbey by sunset."

"What you say is very interesting," said Sir Pressitt smoothly, ignoring the hurry. "But how do I know your story's true? You might be an escaped lunatic making it up. Tell me how you got out of such a well-fortified place."

"What's it to you who I am – or are you willing to help me, take me back to your hall and lend me a horse?"

Sir Pressitt nodded impatiently and the other hurried to croak out his story. "Made use of my wits – persuaded my blind jailor to escape like the other serfs; try to get to a city and become a free man. He promised to saw through my chains and I would guide him. That was the bargain. But I failed in my part of it and left him there, to my shame."

Sir Pressitt looked at his new friend admiringly. "Oh, so you laid him out, once you were free, then abandoned him. Sensible idea, I'd have done the same."

"I'll have you know, I'm a true knight and stick to my given word," cried the other indignantly. "It was an accident. We waited until the castle was empty, everyone out watching my treacherous brother – Devil take his soul."

"I heard something about the combat."

"My prison's like a grave. Well below the level of the moat, dark as night, nothing to hear but the dripping of the water as it runs down the walls and makes puddles on the floor – good breeding place for frogs – swarms with them – kept me company all those years. The blind man came down, set me free, then, in his excitement, forgot about the slimy flagstones, slipped on some stale frogspawn and went over like a felled tree. I couldn't rouse him – couldn't carry him – so there was nothing for it but to leave him there."

"And here you are, safe and sound." Sir Pressitt, finally convinced that the story was true, rubbed his hands together and wondered how much this secret was worth.

"Good to see the trees again – touch the leaves," said Sir Tiff Fide with a sniff, trying to get his eyes used to the bright green light of the forest. Then he suddenly clutched his beard with both hands and stood there listening, quivering like an aspen.

"I can't hear anything."

"They're coming to find me!"

Sir Pressitt hesitated, then grabbed the stick-like arm, bent his head and dived into the thick undergrowth, dragging his companion after him.

"Today's been nothing but one disaster on top of another," complained Sir Charge, furiously pushing his way through the nettles. "We'd no sooner carried Sir Taxe up to the castle, than we saw all the doors leading to the prison

59

standing wide open and discovered the blind serf lying on the stones surrounded by blood and broken crockery. How did the mad man get free of his chains in order to attack his jailor, that's what I want to know."

"Seeing as how he's possessed of the Devil, then the Devil's magic could have gone and helped him to escape," reasoned Hugo First, keeping carefully behind Sir Charge. "Did you hear how that blind man swore when he came to his senses? Chilled my blood, it did. Called him every name in Hell. Said he was evil, violent, mean and treacherous. The most crafty warlock ever held behind bars."

"I don't know who to look for," said Sir Charge, viciously slicing off the head of a foxglove. "He must be tall and strong as an ox to give the serf such a crack on the head with the heavy water jug. But that's all we have to go on, and it's not easy to recognize a man you've never seen."

"Or a Devil – in which case I'm not over-anxious to find him." Hugo First gave the hollow willow tree he was passing a half-hearted bash with his sword and gasped as a startled rabbit ran out. "Sir Taxe knows best, and he says a man could die of fright if he so much as looked at the prisoner's face – that's why he's served by the blind serf. I'm as good a soldier as any, but I'd rather not put Sir Taxe's warning to the test."

60

"Fool's talk," muttered Sir Charge. He walked thoughtfully round a clump of trees, then looked back the way they had come. The heads of the garrison soldiers could clearly be seen above the undergrowth. They were spread out, beating the bracken with the flat of their swords. "We'll never find him this way. Send someone back for a couple of hounds. If we give them a sniff of the foul air in the prison, they'll soon scent him out."

Meanwhile Sir Pressitt was dragging Sir Tiff Fide through the long grass and then, looking over his shoulder at the flattened trail, pulled him some way through the hawthorn bushes; but that only left tell-tale shreds of rags on the sharp twigs, so they returned to the open. Sir Pressitt jumped to conclusions as he rushed along.

"Ha, I see it all. Fifteen years in prison brings us back to the year following Poitiers. Having survived the battle, you came home to claim your estates, at which Sir Taxe – not wanting to give them up – had you waylaid and flung into prison. Yes, it was about that time that he let it be known that his brother was dead."

"We met in the forest," panted Sir Tiff Fide, jerked off his feet and being towed along so fast they were getting left behind. "When he saw who it was, he cried 'lay hands on that man. He's a warlock. He's got the Devil's mark on him . . . look . . . he's stolen an innocent child . . . carried her off for his foul practices.' He summoned his men . . . burly fellows . . . too young to remember me . . . had me gagged and bound . . . carried home in a sack . . . smuggled into the cell. Can't say any more . . . out of breath; but you'll get your reward . . . once we get to the Abbey."

"I'll get my reward all right," Sir Pressitt muttered. "But I haven't got the full story yet – not by half." He stopped to listen. Sir Tiff Fide's lungs were making a terrible noise, but the forest was uncannily quiet and still; the leaves

hung on the trees without moving. "The chase must have been called off, so we're safe for a while." They settled down for a rest in the shade of an oak tree with their feet in a dried-up ditch. Sir Pressitt went on with his interrogation mercilessly.

"You've not been seen or heard of in these parts since I was a boy. Where did you live all those years before Poitiers?"

"I was a soldier . . . well known in France," said Sir Tiff Fide proudly, struggling for breath. "Joined King Edward's army in 1337 . . . fought in the sea battle of Sluys. Dreadful . . . ships crashing together like thunder . . . armed men dropping into the waves . . . always down, no hope of coming up again. After that, there was Crécy . . ."

Sir Pressitt had no time for military campaigns. "Other knights get leave to come to England, visit their families, see to their estates."

"No I . . . I was needed at the siege of Calais."

"Not too busy for such a short journey."

Sir Tiff Fide shuffled his feet in the dry leaves. "There was the Lady Cinque Tiff Fide at home," he muttered.

Sir Pressitt understood at once. "I remember her. A miserable lady, should have been a nun."

"Married her by mistake – tricked into it. Youngest of five daughters, face like a pie dish and no fortune to go with it. Too much religion: always on her knees, praying to some saint. No. It was better among the soldiers. How they cheered as I went thundering into battle on my great charger, Wyde-Gyrth; how they swore as we hacked our way through the press!" He was standing up, wobbling about on his feet, slashing at the air with a stick; but Sir Pressitt pulled him back on to the bank.

"You had a son," he persisted, struggling to recall the neighbouring household. "The boy was raised at Sterlyng Castle until your wife died of the plague – 1348, or thereabouts."

Sir Tiff Fide opened and shut his mouth, but no sound came out. Pointing to his throat and patting his chest, he showed that he had completely lost his voice. Then he scraped away the leaves at his feet and lovingly scrawled the words "Morte Tiff Fide."

Sir Pressitt nodded, remembering the name. Then he felt under his tunic and brought out a small leather bottle that had hung on his belt. He drank most of the wine himself and then handed the bottle to his companion, who hurriedly finished off the rest.

"That's better," the voice came back in a whisper. "Haven't tasted Burgundy wine since Bordeaux. That's where I was, serving with Prince Edward of Woodstock, when my son sailed out to join me. Glorious life: fighting and feasting – wine flowing like water – used it for the fountains. Haven't any more, have you?"

Sir Pressitt said he hadn't.

"My boy Morte Tiff Fide was a great favourite with the prince: called him the handsomest youth in his army . . . dubbed him a knight as soon as he set eyes on him. Found him a wife too, from King Pedro's court. Berengaria Uracca, they called her, but I never could pronounce it. Not cast in the same mould as my wife; wonderfully fair and lively as a cricket. Sang like a lark on a summer's day. I had a squire then, a clever lad, I recollect how he used to accompany her on his lute." The wine brought back all the old memories and tears started trickling through the tangled beard. "Me and my boy fought side by side, always in the thick of it: battles and forays; raiding towns, taking castles, spoiling cities, burning villages and laying waste farmland like any Christian soldiers. Never seen booty to match it: jewels, silks, enamel caskets, silver candlesticks, gold crosses, tapestries, ivories, relics of saints a-atichoo!"

The old warrior's mind had travelled a long way from the forest, but as the echo of the sneeze died away, he was brought back to reality by the faint, far note of a hound giving tongue.

"They're after me again. They're going to track me down like a beast!"

"Then, like a beast, we must look for water." Once again, Sir Pressitt took hold of the skinny arm and raced the quarry along the ditch, following its twists and turns; then left it, hauling him up a bank and flinging him over the sandstone ridge so that they both rolled down into a deep narrow gorge with a brook bubbling along at the bottom. They waded some distance upstream, then climbed, dripping, up the steep bank to the undergrowth at the top. The cry of the hounds was clearer now, and Sir Pressitt realised his time was nearly up.

"What became of your son?" he insisted as he plunged through the saplings, towing Sir Tiff Fide behind him like a ragged sledge; the old man having lost his feet altogether.

"Killed at Poitiers," he sobbed as he bumped along. "Dragged from his charger – ouch – slain before my very eyes. The last thing I remember – ooh – before the terrible bang."

Sir Pressitt stopped and looked down at Sir Tiff Fide, leaving him sprawled on the long grass.

"I was given such a blow on the helm with a mace, I thought my head had exploded. After that, my mind's a blank."

Sir Pressitt made no attempt to help his companion to his feet, but folded his arms as if to show he was no longer interested. "Well, it looks as if I've got the whole story. I'm disappointed, it's not as good as I'd hoped. You weren't killed at Poitiers, but probably lost most of your wits with that blow on the head. I'm not surprised Sir Taxe keeps you locked up. I'd have done the same in his situation. I must be going."

Sir Tiff Fide crawled forward and clung to his feet, pinning him down. "But you promised to save me."

Disengaging himself with a couple of well-placed blows, Sir Pressitt started to stride away through the trees.

"If you won't help me – then at least champion her cause!"

He turned sharply and came back. "Whose cause?"

"My little grand-daughter, Myste Tiff Fide."

Sir Pressitt gaped, then grabbed the old man by the neck and lifted him up, right off his feet.

"Why didn't you tell me your son had a child and that child was Myste?"

"You didn't ask."

"If the father was dead, then what became of the mother?"

"She died when the baby was born."

They could hear the tentative notes of the hounds

65

MYSTE'S FAMILY TREE

MYSTE TIFF FIDE
1357–

SIR MORTE TIFF FIDE
1334–1356
HANDSOME COURTLY
AND COURAGEOUS.
m.
LADY B.U. TIFF FIDE
1336–1357
NAMED BERENGARIA URRACCA
AFTER THE DAUGHTERS OF
ALFONSO VIII. SPANISH AND
VERY BEAUTIFUL.

SIR TIFF FIDE
1310–
m.
LADY CINQUE TIFF FIDE
1318–1348
FIFTH IN A FAMILY
OF GIRLS. A PLAIN BUT
SAINTLY WOMAN. DIED
OF THE PLAGUE.

SIR TAXE
1320–
m.
LADY SUPER TAXE
1345–

MANY LITTLE TAXES WHO DIED IN INFANCY

SIR TIFF FIDE TAXE
1266–1321
A GOOD STOUT VALOROUS
KNIGHT UNTIL HE
MARRIED LADY CRIPPLING,
WHEN HE WENT ALL
TO PIECES. SETTLED
DOWN TO RAISING
SHEEP AND BUILT
STERLYNG CASTLE.
ADDED TAXE TO HIS NAME
TO MAKE IT SOUND
MORE ENGLISH.

m.

LADY CRIPPLING TAXE
1289–
A GREAT BEAUTY IN HER
YOUTH, SHE WAS RENOWNED
FOR HER SCANDALOUS
BEHAVIOUR AT THE COURT
OF EDWARD II. WIDOWED
THREE TIMES IN SIX YEARS,
SHE ACCEPTED
SIR TIFF FIDE WHEN
NO ONE ELSE DARED
TO MARRY HER.

SIR TIFF FIDE OF THE WELSH
1240–1300
ABANDONED LLEWELYN AND JOINED
KING EDWARD I IN 1282. GOT RICH
THROUGH SHEER DISHONESTY.

picking up the scent as they nosed along the muddy banks of the brook.

"Proof," yelled Sir Pressitt, shaking the escaped prisoner as if the words could be rattled out of him like dried peas from a bag. "If I'm to help her, I need proof that you came back to England, bringing her with you."

"It's all written in the records of Hardkipp Abbey," gasped the other, nearly strangled, in a thin, squeaky voice. "My squire and I – lodged there – with the baby."

"So the squire's in the secret as well?"

"Best witness there is, if you know where to find him."

"I think I've got all the information I need." Sir Pressitt dropped the old man and rubbed his bony fingers together. "So poor little orphan Myste isn't a foundling after all, but heiress to Sterlyng Castle and all the rest of the huge family fortune."

"She should be wonderfully rich – help her to get it."

"I will. I will indeed, for what's hers will rightfully belong to the man that she marries." Satisfaction beamed all over his face.

The hounds came racing towards them in full cry.

"They're here," cried Sir Tiff Fide, hobbling in terrified circles.

"So they are," said Sir Pressitt, fading into the bushes.

"Don't leave me!"

But Sir Pressitt was gone.

VI

HOW SIR TAXE NEARLY DIED OF SHAME AND HOW MYSTE WENT SHOPPING AND GOT CARRIED AWAY

The morning following the combat found Sir Taxe lying in his bed, apparently lifeless except for his breathing. He was dressed in nothing but a nightcap and was warmly wrapped in scarlet wool blankets. He wasn't really hurt at all – apart from a few bruises – but his pride had received such a blow, he thought he would never get over it.

Sir Taxe looked exactly like a stone effigy lying in a tomb, for his bedstead – unlike those of other nobles – was a huge, carved, wooden structure that would have been splendidly at home in a church. It was unique. A rich man's frolic. In fact Sir Taxe himself had drawn out the design on a plank of wood and his carpenters had made it up. He was immensely proud of it.

Father Off sat on one side of the bedstead, reciting a bad imitation of the sixteenth psalm, while Lady Super sat sewing at the other, wondering if Sir Taxe was going to die, and if he did, what her chances would be of getting a new husband. Old Lady Crippling was in a high state of worry, continually hobbling in and out of the great chamber, while Lady Ida Dora, bored to death, sat in the ladies' bower next door with her hands folded in her lap, gazing from the window into the empty courtyard below.

68

There was a profound silence in Sterlyng Castle. The
guests had all gone and the servants walked softly and
talked in whispers. Deep down in the prison under the
garrison store room, Sir Tiff Fide tried to keep himself
warm on a pile of mouldy straw, muttering, shivering and
sneezing from time to time. Up above, Sir Charge congratulated himself on having re-captured the prisoner so
promptly, while Sir Taxe had been too ill to get wind of his
escape.

Lady Crippling and Lady Super had had a violent
quarrel the night before and were hardly on speaking terms.
Each was convinced she knew twice as much as the
other about the art of medicine and healing, based on a
thorough understanding of the stars, and the various
properties of plants and small creeping animals. The ladies
had gone out at different times and in different directions
to gather their herbs, snails and such-like things by the
light of the full moon – a lucky omen. The argument had
started just as soon as Lady Super had caught sight of the
contents of Lady Crippling's basket.

Sir Taxe shuddered inwardly as he listened to their
terse remarks; and was even more upset when he overheard his mother sending for the village barber and realized

69

he was about to be bled. He seriously considered getting well again; but his courage failed when he thought of all the shameful things they would say about the combat. Anything was better than having to discuss *that*, he decided.

"The swoon's caused by too much blood pressing on the brain," declared Lady Crippling, smiling grimly as she watched over a pint of it dripping from Sir Taxe's limp arm into a basin.

"People are bled to soothe them and send them to sleep," sulked Lady Super. "I thought we were trying to wake him up."

After the barber had left, Lady Crippling dipped a handful of wool in the juice of fennel and held it to her son's nose.

"This'll rouse him – never fails," she said.

But it did fail, and the old dame, worried and disheartened, went back to the kitchen.

The moment the door was shut, Lady Super hurried to the ladies' bower where she had left her basket of herbs lying on a chest. She chopped green rue, added a pinch of mustard seed, whipped it all together with the white of an egg and then quickly smeared the mixture all over Sir Taxe's forehead with a feather.

"Deo magnifico . . . Nil desperandum . . . misericordia captus, sanctum sanatorium et rigor mortis," chanted Father Off, delighting in the sonorous words. "Cave canem. Amen."

Ignoring the voice, the patient kept his eyes obstinately shut, hardly noticing the strong smell of the rue. He was haunted by a picture of himself in his tight armour, flying like a bird and then dropping like a stone. He kept on hearing the awful roar of laughter that had followed, and then the crash. What a disgrace! How could he ever stand up and face his friends and servants again! How Sir Prize must be gloating!

Lady Crippling's footsteps were stumping back up the stairs. She was pounding snails and lentils to an oozy pulp in a mortar as she came through the door.

"Adam's bones! What's this poisonous sludge?" she demanded, pointing to the green mask slithering down Sir Taxe's face.

"It'll draw the numbness out of his head and restore him to his proper senses," said Lady Super, greatly offended. "We always use it in the household of my father the earl."

"Rue! I thought as much!" exclaimed Lady Cripping, leaning forward to sniff, while Sir Taxe half lifted an eyelid. Catching sight of the snail mixture, he went completely rigid, clenching his teeth. "Look what you've done! He's been seized by a fit!" With a firm hand, she took her son by the nose, forced his mouth open and spooned the dose into it, making sure that it was swallowed.

Lady Super had her own ideas about a good healing dose and wasn't to be out-done by her mother-in-law. As soon as the old woman had gone, she took up a silver cup, filled it with wine and dropped four large pearls into it.

"What a shameful waste," cried Lady Ida Dora, sweeping in from the ladies' bower to watch the pearls dissolve.

"Anno domini . . . hocus pocus ad nausiam . . ." recited Father Off, happily giving the medicine his blessing.

Sir Taxe suffered another quick seizure. Two-thirds of the wine went down his throat and the rest dribbled down his chin, into his beard.

The next potion from Lady Crippling was a mixture of pennyroyal and pigeon dung: after which Lady Super forced Sir Taxe to swallow a concoction of chopped cabbage, cowslip and powdered earth-worms. Strangely enough, although his wife and mother used every recipe they could think of, nothing could rouse him from his unnatural heavy sleep. Even Theriacum – the universal

71

remedy, otherwise known as Venice Treacle, and the only medicine the two ladies could agree on – had no result. By the time the sun went down, he had swallowed so many different things that he suddenly came to his senses and was sick all over the sheets. After this, he started to be ill in earnest. Lady Crippling was in a panic; she thought her son was going to die.

"Someone will have to go to Fishport and hire the Bezoar from the apothecary," she declared, dragging a small iron-bound chest from under the bedstead and taking one gold noble and thirty silver pennies from Sir Taxe's store of ready money.

Now a Bezoar was a very special thing: a so-called stone, found in the insides of animals. They were extremely rare and thought to have magical healing properties. The apothecary of Fishport was famous for his Bezoar.

Surprisingly, Lady Super agreed that the Bezoar would probably save Sir Taxe's life, but was quick to add she was sorry she couldn't go herself: she couldn't leave her husband's bedside. He might recover and want to speak to her, or he might get worse and need her even more. At this, Lady Ida Dora flung her arms round her dear friend's neck and declared she wouldn't dream of deserting her – even for a day – at this difficult time. So between them, they decided that Myste should go.

"To-morrow's market day at Fishport," said Lady Super, brightening up, "I could do with some white gauze for a new veil."

"So it is," cried Lady Crippling, re-opening the chest and taking out some more money. "We need camphor, cloves, pepper, ginger . . ."

"They tell me there are splendid Italian silks to be bought at Fishport," said Lady Ida Dora, joining the conversation with enthusiasm.

". . . and I need some blue ribbon for a girdle," added

72

Lady Super.

Sir Taxe groaned inwardly as he listened to the ladies making up their shopping list. He was worried about the queasy state of his stomach and decided it was time for a quick recovery.

Myste was anxious about her guardian's strange illness, and said she was willing to do all she could to help. Accordingly, together with the waiting woman, Molly Coddlem and one of the stable boys, she set out for Fishport early next morning. The date was Friday, September 13th.

Molly Coddlem was a practical comely woman, designed by nature in a series of circles and curves which made her several sizes too large for the little donkey she was riding. A round wicker basket clutched underneath her cloak made her look fatter than ever. The donkey, obstinate and distrustful, went along in a series of stops and starts. Every time it came to a halt, the stable boy leant down from his dun-coloured pack horse and gave it a hard blow on the rump, which made the beast scuttle rapidly forward and left Molly Coddlem clinging to the saddle, crying out in vexation and shaking all over like a jelly. Myste trotted behind, sitting straight and proud on an old bony mare.

Molly Coddlem's donkey pattered over the stones of Great Sterlyng village, flicking its ears at the women spinning in the open doorways of their dark windowless huts, and sniffing the vegetables and herbs growing in their gardens. Beyond the village there was a good straight grassy road with Roman foundations, while beyond that, there was nothing solid under the surface of mud and stones; the highway became a mere track, twisting and turning round the tree-covered hills.

"You don't need to tell me we're a-riding over Sir Prize's land!" exclaimed Molly Coddlem, as her donkey tripped and fell into a large hole full of water. "A body could be

73

drownded before he'd care. His road's a disgrace. A danger to all."

This was true. Sir Prize was so interested in hunting, he never noticed the state of his roads. To Myste, however, his land was beautiful because it also belonged to Sir Bastion. The river flowed through Chasemwell Vale under its early morning haze and the oak leaves were turning brown at the edges. She caught a quick glimpse of Chasemwell Hall as her horse clattered over the ramshackle wooden bridge and then it vanished behind the tall trees.

The donkey recognized an ale house at the cross roads and so did the stable boy; but Molly Coddlem refused to dismount, pointing out the peasants drinking their breakfast ale under the apple trees.

"It's nobbut a rowdy place; full of draggled ploughboys and the like. I'd be ashamed to be seen as a corpse in such company."

So the donkey was beaten, and they went on.

The road was filling up, busy with villagers taking spare produce to market, carried on the backs of men, asses, mules and pack-horses. It was loaded on carts of all shapes and sizes; some with nail heads sticking out round the wheels to get a better grip on the muddy roads. There were heavy carts drawn by slow-moving oxen; light wicker carts; home-made carts of rods and rails; and two-wheeled carts drawn by huge dogs. There were farmers on horseback; monks on mules, peasant women carrying bundles on their heads, men with sacks on their backs, boys driving herds of sheep, and lads prodding pigs along with sticks. Molly Coddlem's donkey took a strong dislike to the pigs; it put its ears back and wouldn't pass them. A sudden beating from the stable boy sent it dashing off down the road at a gallop.

"Lord-a-mercy!" gasped Molly Coddlem, clutching the saddle, the basket, and her head veil. "I'll be dead afore we

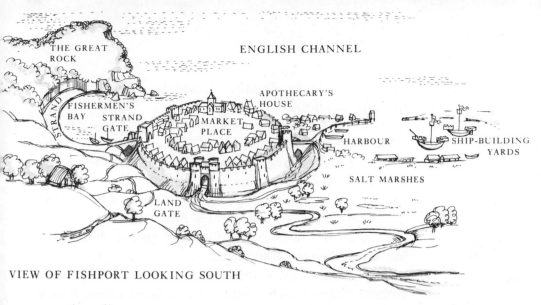

THE GREAT ROCK

ENGLISH CHANNEL

APOTHECARY'S HOUSE

FISHERMEN'S BAY

STRAND GATE

MARKET PLACE

HARBOUR

SHIP-BUILDING YARDS

SALT MARSHES

LAND GATE

VIEW OF FISHPORT LOOKING SOUTH

gets there."

The donkey seized up altogether when it had carried its load to the top of a hill, so they all dismounted, sat on the grass under a hawthorn tree to eat some oat cakes, and stared at the view spread out before them like a map. They could see the road wriggling through the salt marshes like a snake. A high stone ridge bordered the fen to the east, blocking the horizon and ending in a great rock jutting into the sea. Fishport had been built on a bumpy outcrop of this rock which sheltered the town from the cold sea winds. The harbour and ship-building yards at the river mouth, west of the town, were even more secluded.

The king had recently spent a lot of money on Fishport: building strong walls and towers to fortify it against the French. English sailors often took it into their heads to swoop down and sack a town on the opposite side of the Channel; whenever this happened, the enemy was sure to pay a return visit.

However, the war seemed a long way off as Myste, Molly Coddlem and the stable boy finally trotted over the echoing drawbridge, under the portcullis, through the cool dark archway and entered the town.

"In all me born days, I've never been so shook to pieces,"

75

complained Molly Coddlem, painfully lowering herself from the saddle.

Myste slid from the mare's back, smoothed out her creased gown and made sure that the money-bag Lady Crippling had given her was safely tied to her belt beneath it.

Fishport had all the bustle and importance of a town with an expanding trade and more business than it could deal with. Myste and Molly Coddlem left the stable boy and joined the busy throng hurrying up the steep street leading to the market place.

The wooden stalls were crowded together in a small space on the north side of the church. Apart from the local produce, they were piled high with splendid luxuries to be sold to the rich. The two women squeezed through the crowd towards a stall fluttering and shimmering with brilliant silks, imported from Italy.

"Oh – look at that peacock pattern!" exclaimed Myste, with sparkling eyes. "It's worked with such fine gold and purple thread, it's like gossamer!" Then her face clouded. "Silk gowns aren't for me. This time next summer, I'll be walking round a cold cloister wearing a nun's habit."

"Speakin' for mysen, I'd rather spend my days as a waiting woman than a nun."

"And so would I," said Myste with a shudder.

After clever bargaining, the white gauze, five yards of Italian silk, blue ribbon, spices and other goods were successfully bought and stowed in the basket.

Myste had enjoyed herself so much in the market that she nearly forgot about Sir Taxe lying ill. They hurried to the apothecary's shop that was just round the corner from the stalls. It was a large timber-framed house; the lower shutter of the front window let down and, supported on two legs, made a counter. There was narrow roof up above to keep out the rain. The apothecary stood inside the house and asked Myste what she wanted through the window.

76

"I've come to hire the Bezoar," she said. "My guardian, Sir Taxe, is mortally ill."

The apothecary didn't look as if dealing with medicines had done him much good. He had a pasty complexion and spoke down his long nose as if he didn't dare open his mouth in case he caught an infection. "Sir Taxe must be in a bad way if he's sent for the Bezoar," he hooted. Disappearing into the dark room behind him, he returned with a little leather bag hanging on a long chain. Opening the bag, he proudly showed Myste a hard lump of gristle.

"See this? It looks ordinary enough I dare say; but it's magic, so take care. It's as old as the Bible. Came out of the Queen of Sheba's pet monkey, found mummified in the desert. Anyone wearing this Bezoar's wonderfully protected against plague, poison, assault, drowning, sword cuts, burns, starvation, ague, falling sickness, feebleness of the brain, gripe, spasms, hiccups, warts and carbuncles. It'll prevent or cure any illness. Bring it back as soon as Sir Taxe is safely recovered. Someone else is sure to want it."

Myste reluctantly exchanged the gold noble and thirty silver pennies for the Bezoar and hung it round her neck by the chain, privately thinking that she'd made a bad bargain.

Their mission at Fishport being over, Molly Coddlem started searching for the stable boy. It was mid-day. People were celebrating their purchases by eating too much and getting drunk in the taverns. Boisterous music – pipe and drums – interrupted by loud cries of applause, came from the market place, where a famous juggler was performing. The crowd hurried through the narrow streets towards him with all the excitement of a swarm of bees. Soldiers ran down the steps from the town wall and joined the throng

which swept Myste along. Although she tried to make herself taller by running on her toes, she had completely lost sight of Molly Coddlem. A rope had been tied between two trees of the churchyard and the juggler was walking along it, tossing daggers into the air. He was a tattered, greasy-looking young fellow and Myste thought his performance over-rated.

She suddenly got tired of being pushed and jostled by so many noisy people and wanted to be alone. Slithering down a street that seemed to be paved with a mixture of mud and fishbones, she came to the strand gate at the bottom. The road went through and then split into two: one leading inland up the hill; and the other – the strand – curved round a little bay and ended at the base of the great high rock.

Myste followed the strand path, took off her hose and garters, sat on the sea wall and dabbled her feet in the cool salty water. It was peaceful with no one about. Even the fishermen had left their boats and nets and gone to watch the juggler. The breakers broke and rolled; the sun warmed the pebbles; and the gulls swooped and soared. Myste wriggled her toes in the clear water and wondered what Sir Bastion was doing.

Myste sighed. The best part of her life was over; nothing would ever happen to her again, because nothing ever did happen in a convent – except prayers seven times a day. She took another deep breath of the lovely sea air and smelt burning: a cook must have spoilt the dinner. The sea's murmur grew louder and louder and turned into a deafening roar – it was shouting. Turning, she jumped to her feet and stood staring at a huge black pillar of smoke which had lifted itself up from Fishport and was spreading all over the sky. There were bright yellow flames in it, crackling like fireworks. A gigantic bonfire had been lit inside the high enclosing wall and was burning nicely.

78

The gate was jammed with people fighting to get out of it. When they escaped they ran, like a line of ants, away up the hill.

A short round figure, wearing a white veil, hurtled through the dark archway and came panting and sobbing down the strand path towards her. Myste had never seen anyone run so fast. It wasn't surprising. The woman was being chased by a grinning man with a halberd.

"Frenchmen!" Molly Coddlem screamed to Myste. "Run for dear life. There be 'oards of 'orrible Frenchmen." She pointed behind her, tripped on a mooring rope and tumbled over.

"Frenchmen. That's it – and I'll make you cry 'Vive la France' into the bargain!" cried the grinning man, hugely delighted, flourishing the bright weapon about an inch from the white veil. He was stopped in mid-swipe by a loud plaintive cry from the gateway.

"Heula, Pierre About. Stop running after the women. How d'you think I can carry this box single-handed; you know I've a weak heart." A second sailor was dragging a heavy iron-bound chest along by one handle.

"That's your affair, Pierre Below, I'm busy," returned the other, with a significant look at Molly Coddlem.

"Sacrebleu! If you don't lend a hand, you've no right to the treasure."

Pierre About was in a dither; he hated leaving a job unfinished; but he was hard up and needed the money in the chest. He reluctantly lowered the halberd and loped back to his shipmate.

Scrambling to her feet, Molly Coddlem hurried over to Myste and started pulling her along the strand towards the sheer cliff of rock at the end. "Dratted soldiers . . . gawpin' at the juggler . . . instead o' guardin' the wall. Them foreign sinners comed a-ragin' and a-roarin' up from the 'arbour . . . burnin', lootin', killin' at will."

"There's no way out of here," panted Myste. "This path's a dead end. We'll be trapped."

"If we don't hide, they'll be the death of us. Ooh . . . ahh . . . um!"

The scream was snuffed out like a candle by a skinny hand clamping itself over Molly Coddlem's mouth, while a skinny arm encircled her wide waist. A further Frenchman, who hadn't been there before, seemed to have risen like Neptune out of the sea and was squinting over her shoulder. Myste gave one look at this surprising phenomenon, shut her eyes tightly, turned and ran like a blind rabbit until she fell right over the chest that the two Frenchmen were carrying between them. Dropping it with a

80

thump, they grabbed Myste by the hair and sat her on it, holding her tightly between them.

Pierre About grinned, fingering the edge of the halberd.

"Don't cut my throat," begged Myste, in French, "please don't."

"I must, I wouldn't do murder at home; but it's always done on a raid."

The other Pierre sighed, took off his kettle hat and wiped the sweat from his forehead. "Saperlotte, it was 'ot in there. I say you slit 'er throat. I've 'ad enough o' slaughter for to-day."

"You may have; but *I* haven't . . . Diable . . . I haven't had any!" cried the man with the squint, giving Molly Coddlem a playful squeeze. "I've been sitting in the long-boat behind that rock while you've had all the fun. What about me?"

"Here comes Jacques Tour de Force. He'll tell us how to share out the spoils."

A huge, thick-set, bearded, bear-like creature was trundling an immense wine cask along the path, balanced on a wheelbarrow.

"Stop your mouth, Pierre Squinteyes, you've missed nothing. It's been a miserable raid, as raids go," growled the newcomer in a commanding voice. "We was held up by Pierre Below thinking he was having a heart attack; so the other shipmen raced us to the market and took the best of the loot. All they left us was an apothecary's shop, with a cargo of grubs, astrolabes and quack medicines. The two Pierres found that chest under his bed; while I came across this wine in his store room. It's good wine, though, Burgundy best – I sampled it afore carting it away."

"Then I wants my cut o' the goods in the chest and wine in the barrel," declared Pierre Squinteyes. "Fair's fair."

"You can have some o' the groats in the chest, but let go of that fat woman – she's mine," cried Pierre About, pointing an indignant halberd at Molly Coddlem. "I'll swap her for this younger one."

"A good fat wench's a bad exchange for a little thin one. What I'm holding, I'm keeping." Pierre Squinteyes gave Molly Coddlem a vice-like squeeze.

"By all them merciful saints," she gasped, "leave off and I'll tell you someats."

"What can you have to say, chicken?"

"She's a gentlewoman." Molly Coddlem gave a nod in the direction of Myste, still tightly held between the two Pierres, too frightened now to say anything for herself.

"She's not dressed like a gentlewoman."

"That's as maybe; but her hands b'aint rough an' worn as the likes o' me. She lives wi' her guardian in a magnificent castle, all gleamin' wi' white and gold. Sir Taxe'd give half his wealth to get 'er back – that he would." She very much doubted if this was true; but it was worth a try.

"Ha. Something in the nature of ransom money." Pierre Squinteyes stared at Myste as if she might be sold at so much per pound in weight. "You're in command, Jacques. How much would she fetch?"

Jacques turned his dark eyes in the direction of Myste. "It wouldn't be worth it under thirty nobles," the deep voice came rumbling out of the beard. "I'll take ten and you can split the rest between you."

"We'll waste too much time," protested Pierre Below, tired and anxious.

"He's right, we want to get back to France, not dawdle in English waters." Pierre About looked uneasily back at the town. Three more Frenchmen, wearing an odd assortment of armour and carrying a disappointing collection of loot, were hurrying towards them. "Here come the rest of the crew. See how the other ships are setting their sails," he pointed out to sea, beyond Fishport, where four large vessels were rocking on the tide, "We'll be left behind if we don't look lively. Quick, finish off the girls and let's get back to our ship."

"Not so fast," said Jacques, hailing the newcomers and ordering them to fetch the long-boat before turning his attention back to the matter in hand. "We gets our livin' out o' war: raidin', takin' treasure, seizin' prize vessels. We've got nothing but rubbish out o' this trip, so we'll see what price we can get for this lady."

"I'll give my Bible oath, Sir Taxe'll be here along wi' the gold by sunset tomorrow," cried Molly Coddlem eagerly.

Jacques nodded. "Go home and tell your master that his ward's fallen into the hands of honourable Frenchmen, who'll abide by the rules. We'll put to sea, lie out for the night in the channel and return by sunset tomorrow." He pointed a finger at the great rock jutting into the sea. "He's to wait for us on the windward side of that headland: if he plays tricks: if he's late, tries an ambush, or if his coins is short-weight and clipped – we'll sling this here gentle-women over the side and she'll make good food for the fishes."

"Molly Coddlem, you're not going to leave me alone – not with these brigands?" cried Myste, finding her voice.

"Brigands?" echoed Pierre Squinteyes, waving both arms in a typically French gesture. "Who's talking of brigands? I'm as honest a sailor as ever went to sea."

Finding herself released, Molly Coddlem ran to Myste, thrust the two Pierres aside and flung her arms round her neck. "I mun go and there's nowt to do contrarywise."

"No time for sentiment," roared Jacques. "Begone about your business and don't forget the bargain: thirty gold nobles by sunset tomorrow, or this lady's a dead creature – sure as I'm a Frenchman."

Tears streamed down the fat woman's cheeks as she said goodbye to Myste and picked up the shopping basket.

Then, clutching her skirts, she bolted for the homeward road. Arrived at a safe distance, she turned and looked back. The long-boat was being rowed round the headland towards the shore, surging over the choppy waves. Jacques was trundling his barrel towards it, while the two Pierres followed, carrying their chest between them. With a sudden flurry of her threadbare gown, Myste struggled with Pierre Squinteyes; but he quickly bound her with a handy length of rope and slung her over his shoulder as if she was nothing more lively than a sailor's hammock. The barrel, chest and Myste were all stowed in the stern of the long-boat. The men jumped aboard and soon the craft was back at sea, heading for the faint shape of a great ship, lying at anchor just below the hazy horizon.

Molly Coddlem wondered if she would ever see Myste again.

VII

HOW SIR PRIZE AIRED HIS VIEWS ON CHOOSING A WIFE AND HOW SIR LUTE LET SIR BASTION INTO HIS SECRET

There must be some truth in telepathy; for while Myste was dabbling her feet in the sea at Fishport, thinking of Sir Bastion and wondering what he was doing, Sir Bastion was in the great chamber of Chasemwell Hall, describing each of her virtues to his father, who was not a good listener. He preferred to do all the talking himself.

"There are two breeds of women," interrupted Sir Prize, sitting with his back to the window and counting on his fingers. "There's the breed you let yourself admire – usually older than yourself and safely married, like Lady Super. Make yourself as foolish as you like over her, wearing her sleeve at a tournament and all that kind o' nonsense. That's expected of a boy of your age; makes you popular with the ladies. Then there's the other breed: the sort that you don't admire and that's the breed to get a wife from – only way to keep her in her place."

This was disheartening information. Sir Bastion ran his hand slowly down the back of a greyhound, not looking at his father.

"But I love Myste and I want to marry her," he said.

"Love!" exclaimed Sir Prize, screwing up his face as if he was eating a sour apple. "Marriage!" he spluttered,

spitting expertly at the rushes. He abandoned the window seat, rose to his full height and started pacing the room with impressive indignation. "I told you before – but you won't listen – love isn't of the same class as marriage. It's a disease, to be got over, like the plague; but marriage is a matter of business. In marriage, you ask your father to look at the dowry first – the money settlement – and if this is arranged thoroughly to your advantage, you can then permit yourself to take a look at the girl. If she's not to your liking, you can always knock her into a better shape; but you can't alter her fortune. It's goods that count in this life, my boy, not a pretty face. Why, I've seen many a comfortable marriage made out of the most unfortunate features. Look at your own dear mother, God rest her soul, there's an instance . . ."

"Yes father," interrupted Sir Bastion hastily, "but we're talking about Myste, who's different from other girls . . ."

Sir Prize angrily held up his hand.

"Silence sirrah. I'll hear no more about it. The only difference between her and the others is that she has nothing at all to recommend her: no parents, no friends and relations and no *dowry*. A girl without a dowry's a worry to everyone and only good for a convent. You'll have to look somewhere else if you feel in need of a wife and you don't have to look far either." Sir Prize paused to consider. "There's fine quarry near at hand; rich, widowed and a good face – as you're interested in that sort of thing. There's a catch for you, what about her?"

"Who, father?"

"Lady Ida Dora Mann, if she'll take you."

"Lady Ida Dora! Why, she's more than twice my age!"

"What's age got to do with it? That doting old fellah, her last husband, left her with a hoard of gold, furs, jewels, land and the like. They say he only beat her once or twice and left her in fine condition. What more do you expect?"

"I expect my wife to be younger than me – about sixteen."

"That damn fool friend of yours, Sir Tenley. His family's well to do, with plenty of money to spare. Hasn't he got a sister?"

"Yes. There's his twin – Lady May Knotte. She looks exactly like him, which doesn't suit a woman; added to which, she's quite the silliest girl I've ever met."

"So you won't have her?"

"No father."

Sir Prize wasn't used to being contradicted by his son; it riled him and stirred up his temper. Gathering the skirts of his long old-fashioned gown tightly round him, he scuffed through the rushes with his slippers and kicked his favourite greyhound which was trying to sleep.

"Well, what do you want?"

"I want to marry Myste."

"Impudent puppy – damn you! You'll never wed that

87

pauper as long as I'm alive to stop you," he yelled, spilling his temper all over the room. "For a man mayn't marry without his father's consent, so that's the end of it. You're an ungrateful, bad, disobedient, foolish, selfish boy. If I did my duty, I'd have you beaten, locked up and kept a week without food to teach you a lesson. I won't have that vixen's name mentioned any more under my roof – understand? Marry Myste indeed!"

Having got these feelings off his chest, Sir Prize swept down the stone stairway, marched through the timber hall and slammed the massive front door with such force that all the ancient posts and beams shook in their rickety sockets, tugging at their wooden pegs, creaking and groaning in sympathy.

Sir Bastion listened to the bang with folded arms and a rebellious expression. Then he sighed. He could think of no one but Myste. Her magic name fluttered about in his head, making him dizzy. He had to talk about her and he knew where he could find a sympathetic listener. Calling for his horse to be saddled, he pulled on his boots and prepared to ride over to Knotte Hall and visit Sir Tenley.

Meanwhile a flood of citizens were tramping along the road from Fishport: beggars now, hoping to find shelter with friends in the country. Molly Coddlem carried her basket from group to group, crying out that a terrible Frenchman had tried to chop off her head with a halberd and that Myste had been seized and rowed out to sea. No one wanted to listen, but by the time she had plodded through the flat country and reached the base of the hills, she had done so much talking that her throat seemed to be made entirely of dust. She wanted a drink more than anything else in the world. Her feet had swollen to twice their normal size and stones were coming through holes in her shoes. She stopped talking altogether as the road climbed steeply upwards and took to puffing and panting instead. When she had finally struggled to the top of the first hill she found herself staring at the familiar hawthorn tree they had rested under earlier in the morning to eat their oat cakes. The grass was still trampled and flattened. The sight of it brought on a fresh wave of misery, so Molly Coddlem turned and looked back at the blackened walls of Fishport with the gleaming sea beyond, planted her basket on the grass, sat down beside it and burst into tears.

The crowd passed by without so much as a sideways glance. Every time a horseman trotted up the hill she dabbed her eyes, sniffed and looked to see if it was the stable boy, but there was no sign of him or the donkey. The people started shuffling aside to make way for Sir Bastion trotting up the centre of the road from the opposite direction. The track to Knotte Hall met the Fishport Road at the cross roads, so he had heard all about the raid from the miserable refugees and was now riding to the crest of the hill to see the ruined town for himself. Having stopped and stared for some time, he noticed the bedraggled figure crying under the hawthorn tree and recognized, beneath the tears and dirt, the fat woman who waited on Lady Super. He even knew her name.

"Why, what's wrong, Molly?" he asked kindly.

"Mercy on us . . . fancy askin' what's wrong!" she sobbed. "Murder's wrong for a start. So's burnin' and lootin' and bustin' into houses . . . layin' into honest folk inside and carvin' them up like so many cheeses . . . a sight somethink cruel."

"It must have been terrible," sympathized Sir Bastion.

Molly Coddlem nodded her head vigorously and broke into a veritable roar of weeping. She blew her nose with her fingers and wiped her fingers on the end of her long veil, using the other end to dry her eyes. "And you haven't heard the worst on it yet. Them murderin' heathens have gone and clapped hands on poor gentle Myste – wots never said a bad word about no one and carried her off to their thievin' boat. The Lord knows how they might be treatin' her now – for mysen I can't bear to dwell on it."

Sir Bastion felt as if someone had thrust him through with a sharp sword – in one side and out the other. He jumped from his horse, grabbed Molly Coddlem by the arms and shook her until she had rattled out every detail of the pact with the Frenchmen. Then he stopped a passing ox cart, helped her to climb into it, mounted again and rode beside her until they arrived at the inn at the cross roads – the same place that she had vowed never to be seen dead in. She sat under the apple tree clutching a pot of the best brown ale while he went in search of someone belonging to Great Sterlyng village.

People were squashed together inside the inn like salt herrings in a cask, with the ragged juggler standing head and shoulders above them because his feet were on a bench. He was boasting about the way he had used his sword against the Frenchmen, twirling it round as he spoke, flinging it up and catching it. (He did not say anything about how he had been chased three times round the church, crawled under the market stalls, escaped to the town wall, let himself down by a length of fine Italian silk, rolled into the ditch and escaped more quickly than anyone.)

Sir Bastion gave a sharp look round and noticed Sir Taxe's miller – who had left Fishport before the raid and never saw a single Frenchman – listening to the juggler with a look of wonder on his broad red face. Calling the fellow outside, he told him to carry Molly Coddlem back to his master as fast as his mare could travel. Soon half a dozen hefty ploughboys were heaving her up to the pile of empty sacks at the back of the saddle.

"Dratted varlets – I'm not a load of barley!" she complained in her flustered way, pulling her skirt straight and taking a tight grip of the basket. "I'll never want to see another day like this – never. It's made me all of a tremble."

The miller urged his mare to a shambling trot and, with Molly Coddlem bumping behind him, they both disappeared down the road in the direction of Sterlyng Castle. Sir Bastion set spurs to his horse and rode home at a furious gallop.

Arrived at Chasemwell Hall, Sir Bastion flung off his horse, rushed into the hall and stood for a moment listening to the sounds of music coming from the great chamber above. Then he went upstairs three steps at a time.

"Ah there you are," said Sir Lute, abandoning his tune as the door opened, "I've been looking for you. You've put your father into the devil's own temper. He says you're a stupid, idle, rebellious boy, and you want to marry Myste."

Sir Bastion opened his mouth to speak but found he had used up all his breath on the stairs.

"I didn't tell him she's the best catch in the district, heiress to all Sir Taxe's gold and estates," Sir Lute continued in the same level tone of voice.

"What!" gasped Sir Bastion. "If he knew that . . . he'd order me . . . marry Myste . . . as quickly as possible . . . before anyone else does. But first . . ."

"Better keep your voice down," interrupted Sir Lute

with a significant look at the wooden shutter that covered a spy hole overlooking the hall below. "We don't want the servants to hear. Come into the chapel, it's a better place to talk." He opened a narrow door at the end of the chamber and they went into a small room, decorated with faded paintings; with a fine stained glass window, a poor sort of altar and a rickety bench set against the wall. They both sat on the bench, one at each end.

"It's time I told you my secret," said Sir Lute in a low voice. "I was squire to Myste's grandfather, Sir Tiff Fide. I knew her father, Sir Morte Tiff Fide. When I wasn't fighting or serving my master, I was sitting at the feet of her mother – Berengaria – making up little songs and poems to please her. I loved her better than any other woman. Between me and God, when I first caught sight of Myste in the forest, I thought she was her mother's ghost."

"Myste's been carried away by the French," said Sir Bastion miserably. "I came here to tell you."

Sir Lute leapt to his feet and the end of the bench flew up like a see-saw, neatly tipping Sir Bastion on to the tiled floor.

"She was at Fishport market when the town was raided this morning. The French burnt the houses and carried off everything they could lay hands on – they captured Myste and are holding her to ransom. She's in terrible danger."

Sir Lute started walking rapidly round the little room; he could never think standing still. "The French will treat her well enough as long as they expect the ransom to be paid," he said at last.

"And if it's not? It's said Sir Taxe lies in bed and hasn't uttered a word since the combat."

"Even if he was well, I doubt if he'd lift a finger to save her. He'll be glad to hear she's been carried away. He won't want to get her back."

"Because she's the heiress?"

Sir Lute nodded. "I'll tell you the whole story. Sir Tiff Fide wasn't killed at Poitiers – that's a treacherous lie – but he came out of the battle so bloody and battered, we knew he'd never fight again. Things went from bad to worse. Sir Morte Tiff Fide was dead and Berengaria died the night Myste was born. The servants seized their opportunity, ransacked the house and made off with his treasures; while his friends avoided him as if he had the plague. I was the only one left to dress his wound, prepare food, buy wine and hire a nurse for the baby. By the time he could travel, we were so poor, we could hardly pay for the journey home. The nurse wouldn't leave Bordeaux, so our last few groats went to the sailor's wife who cared for the baby on the ship. We were in a sad state when we landed at Hythe," he smiled grimly. "Proud Sir Tiff Fide the Bold returned to his native land a broken-down rusty knight carrying a baby on his saddle-bow and attended by a ragged squire. Even the squire abandoned him in the end."

Sir Lute stopped walking about and stared up at the coloured glass in the window. They could hear Sir Prize doddering about in the yard below, angrily kicking a chicken out of the way and cursing his favourite dogs.

"We spent the night at Hardkipp Abbey – it can't be far from here, on the other side of the forest. The hospice was crowded, sleeping three or four in a bed. When I got news of my family, and heard that my father had met with a hunting accident, I wanted to hurry home and get his blessing before he died. Sir Tiff Fide was looking strong and cheerful, he said he could easily finish his journey alone. I was on the road before daylight and never saw him again."

"He was probably attacked and murdered by robbers – there are plenty of them in the forest," cried Sir Bastion excitedly, "then Sir Taxe came along and found the baby

93

abandoned, as he says."

Sir Lute shook his head. "No one would rob Sir Tiff Fide of his battered armour, it wasn't worth it; and as for his horse, Wyde-Gyrth, his ribs were sticking out like prison bars. His great sword, Slyce-em was the only thing worth taking. But he was still the rightful owner of Sterlyng Castle and Sir Taxe would rather see him dead than riding home to claim it. If he murdered his brother, as I suspect, then Myste would always have weighed on his conscience – a weight that the French have removed."

"Then how can we save her?" Sir Bastion looked desperately round the shabby little chapel. "How can we find thirty nobles at such short notice?"

"Who's talking of paying good money to the French?" demanded Sir Lute with sudden gaity. "There are better ways of getting her out of this wooden ship. We'll watch Sir Taxe to see what he does, and if he won't ransom Myste, then we'll bring her back ourselves. It'll be an adventure. Listen, I've already thought of a plan . . ."

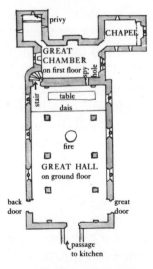

Plan of CHASEMWELL HALL

94

VIII

HOW SIR PRESSITT RODE OUT TO PRESS HIS SUIT

When Sir Bastion said he had better marry Myste before anyone else did, he showed a lot of good sense; but he should never have wasted valuable time talking about her. A rival was up and doing. He was almost too late already.

It had been Friday, September 13th all over the country. The same sun that had witnessed the sack of Fishport and glinted on the bleached wooden shingles at the top of Chasemwell Hall, shone down on the trees of the forest and caught glimpses of a weird-looking horseman travelling under the branches, taking the track to Sterlyng Castle. It was Sir Pressitt.

There was something strange about Sir Pressitt. It wasn't his faded old-fashioned tunic – the only one he had – which he wore every day; nor was it the grubby green hood thrown back on his narrow shoulders. It was his hair. Thin, spiky and hardly ever washed, it stood away from his grim face in corkscrew curls that contrasted oddly with his stiff moustache. Most men would have worn a beard as well; but Sir Pressitt took no notice of fashion and had summoned the barber to scrape his chin before leaving Castle Skint, where he lived.

Sir Pressitt had smartened himself up because he was

on his way to ask for Myste's hand in marriage; and Sir Prize would have approved of the way he felt about her, for he thought of nothing – nothing at all – but the dowry.

"It was a rare piece of good luck, that meeting with Sir Tiff Fide," Sir Pressitt told himself over and over again as he rubbed his bony hands together. "And what's more, the old fellow was speaking the truth." Sir Pressitt, always a cautious sceptical man, had ridden to Hardkipp Abbey and persuaded the monk at the hospice to look up the accounts for the year 1357. There, sure enough, was the name Sir Tiff Fide; set beside the cost of the food he had eaten and the farthing spent on groats and milk for the baby. Evidence to show he had come back to England instead of being killed at Poitiers.

"This secret's worth more than a pile of gold – it'll make my fortune," rejoiced Sir Pressitt, trotting merrily along and stuffing his head with schemes of how to spend Sir Taxe's money. He thought of Castle Skint and his dismal hall in the great grey square keep: There were deep cracks in the stonework and the plaster was falling away in lumps. He would hang those high walls with tapestries woven specially for him, depicting the better exploits of his Norman ancestors. The horse slowed to a careless amble as its rider's fancy dwelt on the long greasy table where he always took his solitary meals. Without so much as wiping away the crumbs, he loaded it with steaming great joints of assorted meats served on dishes of solid gold. A yellow-haired squire was pouring wine out of a gold jug into his gold goblet. He dreamed up gold all over the place and saw himself at the middle of the table, dressed in a gold brocaded gown, putting a large lump of meat into his mouth at the end of a gold-handled knife. There, sitting beside him, sharing his feast was the figure of a sixteen-year-old girl – Myste.

"By all the fiends in Hell. I hadn't thought of that!".

Sir Pressitt halted his horse and quickly passed his hand over his eyes to cancel the vision. What would it be like, living with a wife?

"Horrible, I should think," he cried, turning his horse smartly about and setting off for home at a fast trot. The trot slowed to a jog, followed by a stumbling walk. Then the horse stopped altogether, put its head down and began to crop the grass.

Sir Pressitt cracked the joints of his fingers one by one and discussed his problem with the listening trees. "I mustn't be foolish and throw away this splendid opportunity. Let's consider the situation carefully; I've no money, no goods, no credit, nothing much in the store rooms, and soon I'll have nothing to eat. I was born under an unlucky star: all my father left me was the custody of a decaying castle and a pile of debts. Something's got to be done. If I married this heiress, I could live in comfort."

Having persuaded himself, Sir Pressitt turned his horse with a prick of the spur and set off once again in the direction of Sterlyng Castle. The further he rode, the more miserable he became. He was haunted by visions of Myste flitting up and down the dark stairs of his keep like a butterfly in a cave. She would want to alter everything; turn his gloomy rooms into places that were bright and tidy, with well-scrubbed floors. Sir Pressitt began to feel sick with worry and stopped his horse again.

"Lucifer! How can I claim the dowry without actually having to marry the girl?" The answer was that he couldn't, so Sir Pressitt's highly-strung imaginative mind split right down the centre and divided into two.

"I won't marry her," declared Sir Pressitt number one. "It's too much of a sacrifice."

"What's the point of discovering a secret if you don't use it?" argued Sir Pressitt number two.

"There's no place for a woman in my castle," said number one. "How would you like to live shackled to this girl?"

"Shackled? I wouldn't be shackled. I wouldn't even see her. The proper place for a wife is upstairs, under the roof, next to the battlements," argued number two persuasively.

"That's a very good idea," cried number one, much relieved. "You show good sense with that remark. I could forget all about her if she was locked up there. It's the coldest place in the castle: the wind's always blowing a gale and the rain comes right through the tiles. I doubt if she'd survive the winter."

Having finally made up his mind, Sir Pressitt pulled himself together, set his bewildered horse in motion and hurried on his way to Sterlyng Castle. The sun was sinking and it was getting late.

Meanwhile Sir Taxe sat in his great carved wooden bedstead, a pile of soft cushions at his back and his eyes wide-open, bright and alert. The dreadful medicines had cured him: he didn't want to swallow any more and so had decided to recover. He made up his mind to be in the best of health before Myste arrived home from Fishport. Not that the Bezoar was too awful in itself; but the apothecary might have given her some other vile potion to bring with it. Better to be on the safe side.

The three ladies of Sir Taxe's household had congratulated him on his recovery, then seated themselves on the wide bench that was part of his bedstead and chatted across him as if he wasn't there. He felt cornered. Time dragged on and he found he was suffering from such an acute sense of boredom that he actually challenged his wife to a game of chess. Having won in four moves, he resisted the temptation of breaking the board over her elegant head, but flung the pieces at her instead. They rolled over the floor and got lost among the rushes. This show of temper did him a power of good, made him feel more of a man. He would show them who was master of the house! Lady Crippling and Lady Ida Dora quickly found excuses to leave the room.

"Pick up the pieces and put them back in the casket," ordered Sir Taxe, determined to keep up the bullying.

Lady Super shot him a sulky glance, then obediently collected the little carved figures. She was still searching for the queen when she heard angry voices coming through the open window of the ladies' bower.

"You are the porter, so why don't you open the gate?"

"Sir Taxe is a-bed and won't see no one."

"What's your name?"

"Peter Doubt," said the porter reluctantly.

"I'll tell your lord that Peter Doubt's a surly rascal who does his job badly."

"Orders is orders and I does as I'm told."

Sir Taxe pricked up his ears and listened with keen interest. "That high rasping voice sounds like Sir Pressitt," he said in surprise, knowing that Sir Pressitt never went anywhere. He was the only man Sir Taxe could think of who hadn't watched his performance at the combat; the only man he could face without shame. A business talk would help to pass the time. "Go to the gate and tell Sir Pressitt to come up," he said to his wife.

Lady Super had a low opinion of Sir Pressitt: she looked down her long nose and did as she was told reluctantly. As she went downstairs, crossed the hall and came gliding out of the main door, she decided to forget the humiliation of the chess game by showing Sir Pressitt what she thought of him. The courtyard was already in deep shadow. She swept over the dark cobbles with the supple movements of a great lady: skirts tucked under her elbow, shoulders back, chin in, stomach out and greeted her visitor with all the warmth of a January icicle.

"God prosper you. My lord sends greetings and will see you in the great chamber."

Sir Pressitt unbuckled his sword and dagger, led his horse through the dark passage of the gatehouse and handed the weapons and reins triumphantly to the porter, who looked for the stable boy, who wasn't there.

"Stupid idle flat-mouthed varlet," he grumbled, feeling badly let down by Sir Taxe and wanting to abuse someone. "He's a-dawdling at that there inn, instead of comin' straight home from Fishport. I'll 'ave to stable the horse mysen."

Lady Super was succeeding in making Sir Pressitt feel uncomfortable. She scrutinized him in a way that made his hair uncurl and stick out at odd angles; his tunic got greasier than ever; and his hose suddenly slipped down and wrinkled themselves round his ankles. His shoes felt so down at heel, he wanted to kick them off and lose them in a dark shadow. Setting his mouth in a grim line, he followed the elegant figure across the courtyard and promised himself that one day all her things would be his.

With this idea uppermost in his mind, he carefully inspected the tapestries hanging in the great hall – made in Flanders from Sir Taxe's own wool. The high table was laid for supper, there were maple-wood bowls ringed with silver gilt; gold drinking cups, ivory-handled knives, all placed on a pure white pleated cloth. There was an immense silver-gilt salt cellar, a ewer shaped like a knight on horseback, and two heavy candlesticks, crawling with tiny figures. (Without banks, rich men turned their money into gold and silver ornaments which could always be melted down if need be.)

As Lady Super preceded him up the stairs, Sir Pressitt's eyes fixed themselves on the little gold sheep embroidered all over her gown. They went rippling up the steps like a frightened flock being chased by a wolf up a hill. They were a good omen. For a moment they disappeared into the dark shadow as the stairs spiralled round, then ran gleaming back into view, brightly lit by the window at the top.

Lady Super stood in one of her best attitudes, one hand laid lightly on the latch of the door.

"Remember that Sir Taxe has been mortally ill. Please make it a short visit, speak softly, and on no account rouse him to anger."

Having said this, she opened the door.

Sir Pressitt took one step inside the threshold, then stopped rigid as if a spell had been cast on him. His mouth gaped. His eyes started from their sockets and took in every detail of the magnificent bedstead. They crept up the clustered corner pillars and went revelling among the ornamented pinnacles that sprouted at the top like a crop of young fir trees. Right at the summit, almost touching the

ceiling, they encountered an equestrian statue of Sir Taxe
himself in silver armour.

"I notice you're surprised," said Sir Taxe complacently,
waving up at the carved canopy above him. "I designed it
myself."

Sir Pressitt's eyes came down from the ceiling, looked
past Sir Taxe, and explored the panels just behind him:
they were painted with pictures showing interesting
moments in the life of Saint Etheldreda and were bordered
by bands of ivory inlay, gleaming with gold, silver and
precious stones. "It looks like a shrine," he gasped.

"It was inspired by a shrine," said Sir Taxe, caressing
the wood and admiring the bedstead himself. "Now don't
be over-awed. Come straight to the point and tell me your
business."

Sir Pressitt's thoughts were jumping about like excited
fleas, he couldn't collect them. The beadstead was magic –
pure magic. A man only had to lie inside this rich frame-
work and he looked like a king. It was the extravagant
symbol of all the wealth Sir Pressitt hadn't got and he

wanted it desperately.

"Come on, you're keeping me waiting," said Sir Taxe.

Sir Pressitt concentrated on the matter in hand. Putting his hand in the place where his heart should have been, he said simply: "You have a ward called Myste. I need a wife. I have come to ask for her hand."

"Your request," said Sir Taxe in an amused, deliberate voice, "is a cartload of rubbish."

Sir Pressitt thought there must be something wrong with his hearing. Sir Taxe wasn't acting according to plan. In view of the secret, he should be delighted to get rid of his embarrassing ward.

"It's rubbish," continued Sir Taxe, "because I don't intend Myste to marry you or anyone else. She's a good, obedient, religious girl; with just the right voice for singing psalms. She's got a vocation: she likes sitting quietly for hours on end and thinks before she speaks – a rare virtue in a woman. My mother needs someone to pray for her after she's dead. Myste's going to be a nun."

"What a waste!" exclaimed Sir Pressitt, before he could stop himself, thinking of the money she ought to inherit.

"A worse waste to give her to you," returned Sir Taxe, also thinking of his money: Myste was safer in a convent. "Anyway," he continued, feeling his power and enjoying himself, "If she were to marry – which she's not – I'd choose a man of wealth and high standing: I wouldn't throw her away on a nobody."

"A NOBODY!" hissed Sir Pressitt.

"Nobody very important," returned the other smoothly.

Sir Pressitt was shouting at the top of his voice: "I'll make you sorry you ever spoke that word. I'll show you what a nobody can do."

"Hush." Lady Super, who had been eavesdropping, came running through the door.

There was a stir in the courtyard, but Sir Pressitt was

making too much noise for anyone to notice. "Go to the devil," he cried, stamping with rage. "You and your high-stomached ways."

"I told you not to get him excited," shrilled Lady Super.

But Sir Taxe was bouncing on his feather mattress, laughing in Sir Pressitt's face. "Do you think you can hurt me, a poverty-stricken man like you?"

Steps were coming up the stairs.

With a last look at the wonderful bedstead and a sharp glance at the man inside it, Sir Pressitt swung on his down-trodden heel and stalked out of the room. He bumped into Lady Crippling as she came dragging Molly Coddlem up the steps, with a tight grip on her wrist. Sir Pressitt let them pass into the chamber and then, realizing something important was happening, waited in the dark shadow of the stair to hear what it was. Lady Crippling always spoke with a voice like a peacock, and he soon discovered all about the raid on Fishport: how Myste had been carried off by the French, and every detail about the ransom money and how it should be paid.

Sir Pressitt repeated these details to himself as he continued downstairs. He strode rapidly through the hall, crossed the dark courtyard and called for his horse. Riding through the gatehouse, he took note of the defences of Sterlyng Castle. Spurring through the forest, keeping a good look-out for wolves, he began to plot his revenge.

The news of Myste had driven all thoughts of Sir Pressitt out of Sir Taxe's mind. He heaved a deep sigh of relief, settled a cushion in the small of his back, relaxed and shut his eyes to hide his delight.

"We'll have to let the Frenchmen keep her," he said.

Seeing the way the wind was blowing, Lady Super sank on to the window seat and folded her hands. "So sad. Such a dear sweet girl . . ."

She was interrupted by an ear-splitting wail from Molly

Coddlem. "You wouldn't think o' abandonin' Myste to them cruel foreign . . ."

"We are thinking of no such thing, so hold your tongue," cried Lady Crippling, hobbling to the middle of the room and fixing her son with her piercing black eyes. "Sir Taxe will undertake to have her back here, safe and well, before tomorrow night."

"No I won't," expostulated Sir Taxe, sitting bolt upright in bed. "I can't spare the money."

"Yes you can," replied Lady Crippling with terrible severity. "You can spare three times as much, but we'll discuss this matter alone. Girl, you can go." Molly Coddlem ran out of the door and her loud sobbing continued all the way down to the bottom of the stairs. "I want to be *quite* alone," continued the old dame, glaring pointedly at her daughter-in-law.

With an affronted sniff, Lady Super gathered her skirts and followed the waiting woman. Lady Crippling watched to make certain she had really gone downstairs and wasn't listening behind the door, then stalked over to her son's bedside, hovered above him like a thunder-cloud, then stormed words down at him as if they were hail-stones.

"Idle, thoughtless, idiot, dolt. Woodenhead. Ass. Pretending to be ill and frightening me out of my senses. This is all your fault. If you hadn't disgraced yourself over that affair with Sir Prize, I wouldn't have sent Myste to Fishport and this would never have happened."

"Stand back, for God's sake Mother, you're making me deaf."

"Who do you think you are, to say the Frenchmen can keep her?" shrilled the old lady, beating the embroidered coverlet with her stick and raising a cloud of dust. "You're so selfish, you've no consideration for me. I'm nearing the end of my life and my sins weigh heavy on my soul: who's to help it through purgatory now that Myste's gone?"

"Look mother, thirty nobles could hire a whole convent of nuns to pray for you."

"I only need one nun: Myste. Besides, I'm fond of the girl."

Wrapping the sheet hastily round him, Sir Taxe got out of bed and stood on one foot in the rushes like a hairy-legged stork. His new-found manliness was ebbing away and he behaved like a little boy again. He had always been frightened of his mother. His father having died soon after he was born, she was the only parent he could remember; and for fifty years she had been the real power behind Sterlyng Castle. Sir Taxe shifted his weight to the other foot uneasily and felt as if he had been caught stealing apples.

"If you won't ransom Myste and bring her home safely, I'll send for the sheriff and invite him to take a look at that man you've kept buried in the prison all these years."

"You'd never dare to do that!" exclaimed Sir Taxe, turning white as his sheet.

"Of course I dare. Up to now, I've never asked questions about the prisoner: I've been indulgent and let you keep your secret; but it's something shameful, I'm sure. You can't deceive me with stories of devils."

Sir Taxe retreated to his bedstead. "Do what you like with my money," he complained, climbing on to the mattress. "Fling it away on the French," he said as he lifted the blankets. "Squander it all on the church," he muttered as he crept under them. Then he lay back with a groan and pulled the sheet right over his head.

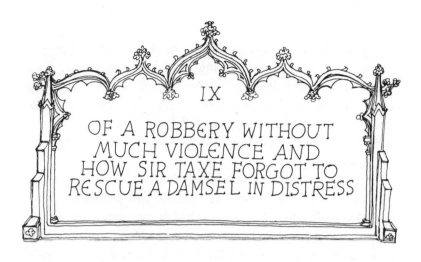

IX

OF A ROBBERY WITHOUT MUCH VIOLENCE AND HOW SIR TAXE FORGOT TO RESCUE A DAMSEL IN DISTRESS

Sir Taxe would never have gone to ransom Myste if his mother had not blackmailed him into it. Next day he made his preparations with bad grace and it was mid-afternoon by the time he was ready.

Even when he was mounted on his horse, he was not in any hurry to leave; but sat fiddling with the leather bag at his belt, chinking the thirty nobles. It would be empty when he came back. He gave Lady Crippling an angry look, then abruptly clattered away through the gatehouse without even saying goodbye.

Sir Taxe had said it was dangerous to travel alone with so much gold; but he privately hoped that – with luck and a little cunning – he might manage to get Myste back without actually handing it over. With this at the back of his mind, he took his entire garrison of soldiers with him. Sir Charge was in command, trotting along on his big-boned horse, while Hugo First marched at the tail end of eight bowmen and twenty footmen at arms.

When they had gone, Sterlyng Castle had all the echoing stillness of an empty church. The steward and other household servants were on the village green at Great Sterlyng, jeering and throwing old eggs and turnips at a baker who was sitting in the stocks, a loaf tied round his neck, convicted of selling short-weight bread. The castle was almost deserted, except for Peter Doubt in his porter's lodge and Father Off dozing in his chapel; while deep down in the prison, Sir Tiff Fide was coughing and sneezing louder than ever, but no one heard him through the thick walls.

Arguing with her son had left Lady Crippling feeling old and tired: she had a sore throat and headache from shouting and listening to herself. She stumped up to the ladies' bower, opened the medicine chest, mixed oil of roses with the juice of peony root, poured it over a linen rag and put the rag on her forehead. Then she lay on the bed, shut her eyes and was soon fast asleep.

The sun slanting to the west lit up the area of courtyard immediately below the ladies' bower; it warmed the chapel steps where the pampered lap-dogs sat scratching and chasing fleas. Butterflies hovered over some wild asters that had been planted between the wall and the cobbles. Lady Super came into the courtyard carrying an enormous bundle, an altar cloth she had been working on for many years. She settled on the bench, unfolded the needlework and began sewing in tiny stitches, while Lady Ida Dora sat down beside her and started carelessly filling in the wings of an angel at the other end.

They would have made a good subject for a tapestry themselves, with the background of purple flowers and red butterflies, hazy in the sunshine.

"Promise to keep my secret?" whispered Lady Ida Dora.

"I'd die rather than breathe a word."

"I've sent a letter to my brother, begging him to find out all he can about Sir Lute's family. If his fortune's half as good as his looks I'll ask him to arrange a marriage between us."

"I thought you'd do something of the sort," said Lady Super drily, snipping off the silk thread with a tiny pair of shears.

Sir Pressitt stood in the middle of a bramble bush, peered through the leaves and watched Sir Taxe and his soldiers march off down the road. When the last man (Hugo First) was safely out of sight, he scrambled out of the bush, tore away a mouldy sprig of berries that clung to his tunic and hurried over to a clump of willows growing on marshy low-lying land at the far side of the moat. A light cart was waiting on the shady side of these delicate trees and with it – lurking in the long grass and rippling shadows – a bunch of sinister-looking toughs. Sir Pressitt always chose servants that were rough, ragged and openly dishonest, and this was the cream of his collection. He had no trouble in persuading them to help with his lawless enterprise. They were agog, spoiling for trouble.

Sir Pressitt surveyed his gang with a grim smile. "I'll enjoy being revenged on that insolent porter, so I'll do the deed myself."

"There's no harm in trying, but you'll not succeed," grinned Ivor Grudge, the reeve, treating his lord man to man as usual, without respect.

"Why not?" demanded Sir Pressitt sharply, thinking his courage was in question.

"On account of that there hairy moustache!" All the men started to snigger.

"Nonsense. Help me with the gown, then hand me the veil and wimple."

Having struggled into a homespun woman's gown, he

wrapped the wimple round his neck and pulled it tight under his nose, while Hugh Woods the carpenter put down the axe he was carrying as a handy weapon and secured the wimple at the top of Sir Pressitt's head with a couple of enormous pins.

"'Ere be thy veil," quoth Hammer Smith, who looked like Noah and who spoke with a voice that came straight from the Bible. He hung the linen over his lord's head like a small grubby tent and tied it round with some cord to keep it in place.

"Tell me thy name, sweetheart," smirked Ivor Grudge, flinging the cloak round Sir Pressitt's shoulders.

"Hold your noise. Where's Willy Doolittle?" Sir Pressitt was breathing through the wimple and his voice was muffled as he peered round for the lad of all work. An eager figure, skinnier and dirtier than the rest, rose up out of a clump of rushes. "Oh there you are. We're all here and there's no need to loiter when there's pleasant work to be done. Let's go."

"How quiet it is," murmured Lady Super, screwing up her eyes and squinting into the eye of her needle as she passed the thread through it.

"Better without the old witch upstairs – just the two of us," whispered Lady Ida Dora, making faces up at the ladies' bower.

"Spiteful old dame," agreed Lady Super.

It was such a delightful afternoon: a bee droned and the butterflies flopped and fluttered among the flowers. The ladies gossiped while Father Off's snores penetrated the chapel door as he slept on a cold wall-seat, his feet propped up on the book of psalms he'd never read.

Outside, a beggar-woman was shuffling crabwise over the bridge towards the gatehouse, bent double with age, rheumatism and a desire to hide her enormous feet.

"Now then, what's this? What do you want?" cried Peter Doubt. Being the only one left to guard the castle, he was doubly wide-awake, doubly conscientious.

"Have pity on a poor old crone," whined the hag, tugging her veil over her eyes with long bony fingers. "All she asks for is a crust of old barley-bread."

"You've come at the wrong time, beggar woman, the time to come is after meals, when they give out the used trenchers." (The rounds of bread, used instead of plates, were thrown into a sack and given to the poor afterwards.)

"I'm faint . . . I'll be dead by supper time."

"That's your funeral. Go away, you lousy old toad," cried Peter Doubt, full of suspicions. "If you need food, you can go and beg in the village."

"My feet won't carry me that far."

"I'd have thought feet that size would have carried you anywhere!" cried the porter in amazement, pointing to the outsize shoes poking out under the gown.

Sir Pressitt thought quickly and bent his knees. "It's the gout that makes them so big. They're worse in wet weather."

"Feet don't grow in the damp like mushrooms."

"Yes they do. With this terrible illness, they get longer all the time."

Peter Doubt didn't know what to believe, so he bent down to take a closer look at the astonishing feet. Sir Pressitt pulled out a mace from under his cloak and gave the porter a cracking blow on the top of his head and he slumped down without a sound.

On the other side of the gatehouse, the lap-dogs had stopped chasing fleas and set up a loud yapping.

"Quiet," Lady Super said severely as she looked up from her sewing.

"They're always barking at nothing." Lady Ida Dora bit off the thread.

"Bring up the cart," roared Sir Pressitt as he flung the gate wide open and was nearly swept off his feet as the excited little dogs gave him a loud welcome.

One moment Lady Super was stitching her embroidery, and the next she was being shoved gracelessly among the butterflies and flowers by Hugh Woods.

"Make way for the cart," he cried, kicking the bench aside. "It's to stand over here."

Lady Ida Dora clasped the half-finished altar cloth to her bosom and expected the worst. "Where's the porter? Where's the chaplain? Who's to protect us?" she shrieked.

The horse and cart rumbled into the courtyard and came to a stop directly under the large window of the ladies' bower. Tearing off the cloak and gown, but leaving the veil and wimple, Sir Pressitt followed.

"Have mercy, have mercy, have mercy," beseeched Lady Super, clasping her hands and shuffling towards him on her knees; but Sir Pressitt passed her by as if she wasn't there and strode on towards the hall. "Hugh Woods and Hammer Smith, bring your tools and come with me. The rest of you wait here with Ivor Grudge," he said as he disappeared through the door.

Lady Super and Lady Ida Dora ran into the chapel chased by nothing worse than their dogs. They swept the candlesticks off the altar and draped the unfinished embroidery over it; then they squeezed round the back to hide under the folds but found that Father Off had got there first. The lap-dogs frolicked round, licking their faces and thinking it was a game; but Father Off complained that the altar wasn't big enough for three.

Meanwhile Sir Pressitt was taking the stairs two steps at a time. He pushed open the door of the great chamber and pointed triumphantly at Sir Taxe's bedstead.

"That's what we've come here to fetch," he said.

Like all good craftsmen, Hugh Woods and old Hammer Smith opened their sacks, sorted their tools and set to work slowly and methodically.

The turmoil below had already half-roused Lady Crippling from her nap; but she sat bolt upright at the sharp tap of a mallet. She got off the bed and stood blinking in the doorway with a worried expression and her head-dress all crooked. Then, recognizing Sir Pressitt, she went into action with the speed of a whirlwind, skirts flying. "What are you doing here, dressed up like a turnip-faced scarecrow in women's clothes," she screamed, attacking him tooth and nail, then trying to strangle him with his wimple. "Scurvey recreant knight – false villain."

"Now stop it Lady, or you'll do yourself an injury," said Hugh Woods, putting down the mallet and restraining her.

"Take your dirty hands off me – serf."

"I will, if my master bids me." At a nod from Sir Pressitt, the carpenter went back to his job of knocking the wooden pegs out of the holes.

Lady Crippling picked up a saw and advanced on old Hammer who was busy prising away one of the corner posts. She was about to saw him in two when Sir Pressitt glanced round and noticed Molly Coddlem's round wicker basket, still full of shopping, lying forgotten in a corner of the chamber.

"You talk so much Lady Crippling, you make me tired," he said choosing the length of blue ribbon. After a fierce struggle, she was bound with the ribbon, gagged with the fine gauze and then firmly lashed to Sir Taxe's gilt faldstool with the five costly yards of Italian silk. After that, she had to sit and watch the bedstead being taken to pieces bit by bit. The sections were lowered through the window of the ladies' bower to the men waiting on the cart below. Some of the timbers were too large, so the smith picked up his sledge-hammer and gave the centre mullion a well-aimed blow. There was no more trouble after that. Even the bundles of bedding were easily tossed through the gaping hole.

Within the hour, Sir Pressitt and his men were on their way back to Castle Skint, having carried off the bedstead, feather mattress, down pillows, cushions, wool blankets, silk sheets, brocaded coverlet and all.

Inside the chapel, Father Off was peering over the top of the altar, listening. "I can't hear anything."

"Have they gone?" inquired Lady Super faintly.

"Are we safe?" Lady Ida Dora didn't know whether to be relieved or disappointed.

They looked into the courtyard and found it empty. The gatehouse was empty too, apart from Peter Doubt sitting on the drawbridge with a bump on his head the size of a swan's egg. Inside the great hall, everything was in its proper place – nothing stolen. The salt cellar and candlesticks were still standing on the high table. It was only when they climbed the stairs and looked into Sir Taxe's chamber that they realized what had happened. They encountered Lady Crippling's angry black eyes and saw her wrapped round in silk bindings like a grub in a chrysalis; they stared at the dusty gap in the rushes where Sir Taxe's bedstead used to stand.

As soon as she was unwound and able to speak, Lady Crippling told Father Off to take Lady Super's palfrey – the fastest horse left in the stable – ride after Sir Taxe and tell him what had happened.

The sun sank down towards the salt marshes, glittering red in the puddles. It left the sky dark on the other side, with little clouds scudding over the windswept grassland of the high stone ridge and the sea beyond. The calm weather was breaking up. The soldiers were tired of marching along the winding road; they dragged their feet through the dust and ignored the yells of Hugo First trying to make them quicken their step. When they heard galloping hooves they all turned, marching like toy soldiers whose heads had been carved back to front.

"Oh calamitas . . . calamitas terribilis . . . calamitas horribilis . . ." came the distant voice of Father Off, perched on top of the light palfrey like a crow in a gale, his black cassock fluttering behind him. "Oh, misericordia . . . oh, magnum scelus . . ." Not having ridden an animal faster than a mule for years, it had been a hard journey. "Impius Sir Pressitt . . ."

"Leave the Latin alone and deliver your news in plain English," cried Sir Taxe, reining in and quickly going through a list of possible disasters.

"Sir Pressitt . . . at the head of a great army . . . raided your castle and carried off . . . carried off . . ."

"Lady Super?" Sir Taxe interrupted hopefully – he could always get another wife.

"No . . . no . . . Benedictus . . . carried off . . ."

"All my gold?" – Not so easy to come by.

The chaplain turned up his eyes to heaven as if the words were flapping about in the sky. "Carried off . . . your bedstead."

"Irreplaceable!" Sir Taxe reeled in the saddle. If Sir Pressitt had chopped off his right hand he could not have dealt a more dastardly blow. Completely forgetting about Myste – abandoning her to her fate among the French – Sir Taxe turned his men about and hurried back to Sterlyng Castle. He was going to make war on Sir Pressitt.

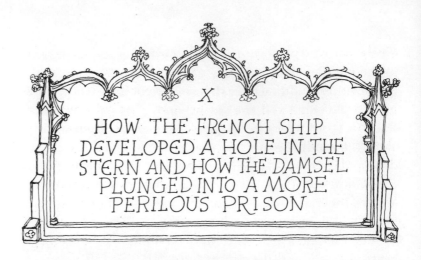

X

HOW THE FRENCH SHIP DEVELOPED A HOLE IN THE STERN AND HOW THE DAMSEL PLUNGED INTO A MORE PERILOUS PRISON

The French ship was a great round tub-like vessel, some seventy feet long and standing high in the water. Fighting platforms had been built fore and aft – the forecastle and the aftercastle – and an eight-pronged instrument called a grapnel hung from a spar at the bow, ready to clutch hold of enemy ships and haul them to close quarters for boarding. There was a stone-throwing catapult mounted on the aftercastle, and piles of stones and iron bars were stored on the deck beneath. There were more stones in the little wooden castle that stood high up at the mast head under the fluttering French flag. The words LE POUR-QUOI PAS? were painted along the hull in thick black letters.

The ship rolled and tossed over the waves in a way that was exactly right for making people sick. Myste, chained to the deck under the forecastle, sat on a goatskin and was successfully ill most of the time. It took her mind off her other miseries.

Showing remarkable spirit considering her timid nature and terrible circumstances, she cried, "I hate you, I hate you all," every time a burly Frenchman came near her.

"Not me, I hope?" inquired the captain of the ship,

116

whose name was Sir Vere de Pression.

Myste looked him up and down with withering scorn. "I hate you most of all."

He was a sad stooping man. It seemed that everything he had done in his life had gone wrong and he had lost interest. He took no notice of the sailors under his command – said they all looked alike to him – and called each one of them Pierre: Pierre About, Pierre Below, Pierre Aloft, Pierre Abaft, Pierre Abeam, Pierre the cook – not forgetting Pierre Squinteyes. The only man who insisted on keeping his own name was Jacques Tour de Force and he really commanded the ship.

"Why does everybody hate me?" complained Sir Vere de Pression, gazing down at Myste and gloomily pulling his drooping moustache. "I'm the most unpopular man alive. What have I done to hurt you?"

"What have we all done?" jeered the crew.

"You're murderers and robbers!" exclaimed Myste. "What right have you to carry me off and put me in chains?"

"England and France are at war – you're part of the loot," Pierre About explained indignantly.

"Anyway, we likes your company," grinned Pierre the cook, handing round salt fish and pease-pudding.

"I won't stay for long," cried Myste, suddenly bursting into tears. "Sir Taxe will soon come and take me away." She was crying because she had no faith in her rescuer.

"Peste, then he's a long time a-coming," Jacques' voice rumbled out of his curly black beard. He pointed his dagger at the sun which had dropped down the sky and seemed to be bouncing on top of a distant rock.

Myste looked helplessly at the red circle. Small clouds hurried past it, driven by a rising wind. There was going to be a storm.

"She's nice," observed Pierre About. "I likes her courage. Tell you wot. If her baron don't come, then I'll take her back to France."

"No you won't. It's me who's taken a fancy to her," cried Pierre the cook, brandishing his carving knife.

"And she won't do that neither." Jacques banged his huge hand hard on the deck. "If she's not ransomed, she's drowned, see?"

"Do as you like with her," said Sir Vere de Pression. "Only kindly leave me out of it."

"Tonnere de Dieu!" cried Pierre Squinteyes, eager to prevent a quarrel. "Jacques, give us another taste of your wine."

The sailors had already been hard at work on the barrel and it was now half empty. It stood near the forecastle, about ten feet from Myste and the wooden bowls were filled up afresh. Sir Vere de Pression replenished his great silver goblet and carried it away to drink alone at the stern of the ship. A lantern was lit and the men settled round it, squatting on the deck with their backs to the prisoner.

The sun dropped behind the rock, leaving a glowing sky. *Le Pourquoi Pas?* rolled over the waves, tugging at her anchor and the wind started to play tunes on the rigging. Myste pulled the dirty goatskin round her for warmth and the men tossed coins to pass the time.

"Heads she drowns and tails she don't," Jacques flipped an English groat and made sure it landed head up.

"Heula!" came a cry from Pierre Aloft on look-out at the masthead. "A light to the starboard bow."

Myste threw off the goatskin and ran over the deck, but was pulled up short by the fetter at her ankle. She stared through the dusk. A flaming brand of wood was waving to and fro at the base of the headland.

The men immediately laced each other into their odd assortment of armour: helms and kettle hats covered their heads and all kinds of knives, daggers, axes and maces were thrust into their belts. Six of them clambered down the rope ladder and into the long-boat that drifted astern, moored to the ship by a rope painter. Jacques stayed behind.

"I should have gone with the boat," cried Myste indignantly, watching it being rowed away.

"We'll hand you over soon as the money's safely aboard," growled Jacques, carefully sharpening his axe with a whetstone. "We're looking for treachery – see? You'll be dead and drowned if your friends try tricks on us – half dead first, drowned after." He ran his thumb up the blade with a grin.

It was very uncomfortable watching Jacques check his weapons and waiting for the long-boat to come back. When at last it came see-sawing over the waves, Myste strained her eyes to identify the extra figure sitting in the stern: it didn't look at all like Sir Taxe or Sir Charge or even Hugo First. It wasn't any of them. She suddenly recognized the tattered hood and gown of the juggler she had seen at Fishport: but that man had been young and cleanshaven; while this was an older man with a beard. Bewildered and disappointed, she folded up on the deck like a glove puppet without a hand inside it, all the courage knocked out of her.

Sir Vere de Pression had been expecting something to go

wrong and was pleased he was right. He hung over the stern rail until the long-boat was directly beneath, then carefully emptied the dregs of his wine into the sea. "All my life, they've given me half-wits to command," he muttered. "Look at them now, go to pick up a rich knight and bring back a vagrant."

"It's not often we have the luck to sail alongside one of these," exclaimed Pierre Squinteyes, jerking his thumb at the newcomer and then scrambling up the rope ladder like a monkey.

"We was tempted . . ." began Pierre About.

"Deceived more likely," growled Jacques, showing his white teeth. "Sacrebleu! I've seen that strange-coloured back before. Ran like a rabbit when I chased it through the streets of Fishport."

"He says he'll entertain us free and for nothing if we see him safe over the channel."

"We've no time to waste on cowardly fools and we'll not have this one aboard our ship."

"This isn't a fool – it's a clever minstrel."

"He's not dressed like a minstrel – more like a juggler. Minstrels come from a better class of people." Jacques was very suspicious.

"The best way to prove I'm a minstrel is to play to you," came the ordinary everyday voice of Sir Lute as he climbed aboard. Myste was amazed and terrified. She stared at him, and the words "You'll be dead and drowned if your friends try any tricks" kept echoing through her head. Clutching her skirts, she crept to the darkest corner of the forecastle, to the end of her chain.

The crew watched her, grinning, while the minstrel picked up the leather bag he carried with him and drew out a beautiful ivory lute. Having pulled a goose quill from his belt and tuned the strings, he sat on the hatch and launched into a rattling good sea shanty which brought smiles to the

surrounding faces and made Jacques slap him on the back
with his great fist and declare he was a proper minstrel
after all. First-rate musicians seldom wasted their time on
common people and Jacques never refused a bargain. Sir
Vere de Pression hurriedly re-filled his silver goblet and
carried it off to the aftercastle. He hated music.

One song followed another and soon the sailors, who
had been drinking wine as if it was water all evening and
were easily pleased, roared out the choruses.

Dark turned to night. Great storm clouds had blown over
the sky and the noise of the wind battering the waves was in
danger of drowning the music.

"Merveille! Superbe!" cried Pierre Squinteyes, ap-
plauding the latest song. "But you know, it's not loud
enough. Hold hard – I'll go fetch my crumhorn."

"Could do with the sound of a fiddle."

"Pipe and tabour as well."

Pierre About and Pierre Below chased Pierre Squinteyes over the fore-deck and disappeared down the trap door.

"I can't play nothing. My fingers are so clumsy, they get in the way of the notes," Jacques confided in the minstrel who wasn't listening. Myste had crept out of her corner and he was staring anxiously at the fetter round her ankle. Jacques swore and looked for his axe.

The three Pierres came lurching back the other way, playing their instruments full blast and falling over Sir Vere de Pression who was trying to sleep. He cursed them, but they didn't care. They were so drunk, they thought the ship was rolling about in time to their music. They took no notice of the gale. They had forgotten all about Myste and the ransom money. They were having a rip-roaring evening and nothing else mattered. The rest of the crew linked arms and they led a dance that got wilder and wilder until the beat of their feet shook *Le Pourquoi Pas?* from stem to stern. The gusty wind picked up the sound and blew it this way and that over the sea in bursts.

"He's done much better than we even dared to hope," Sir Bastion remarked, admiring the noise.

"I wish I was on dry land," moaned Sir Tenley.

"Hand me that rope."

"I've got no faith in this skiff. I say, you might have bought a bigger one from the ship-building yard."

"I couldn't afford one." Sir Bastion was trying to keep his balance and at the same time lash the small boat in which he was standing to the huge rudder of the French ship. His boat lay low in the water, heavy with a mixture of tow, pitch and sulphur.

"I don't trust boats. If you fall off a horse, you hit the ground; but this tub is lurching worse than Passemall and if I fall, I'll sink to the bottom." Sir Tenley looked into the dark swirling water and shuddered. "I wish I was a fish."

122

Sir Bastion's work was finished. He leant out, caught hold of the rope that secured the ship's long-boat and hauled it alongside. Then the two men climbed out of one boat and into the other, which was difficult because the waves were heaving up and down. Sir Bastion took the same brand of wood he had used earlier in the evening to make the signal and lit it, using a flint and steel. Then he leant over and thrust it into the very middle of the pile of sacks. For a moment it looked as if it would go out, then the pitch caught fire and flared up with a sudden sheet of flame. Sir Tenley grabbed the oars in a panic and started to row furiously. He churned up a lot of water, but they stayed where they were, getting roasted.

"Don't be a fool," cried Sir Bastion. "We're still tied to the ship." He cut the rope with his dagger, then they both pulled hard on the oars.

The high rounded stern of *Le Pourquoi Pas?* sheltered the flames from the wind; but it caught the thick smoke and blew it into fantastic shapes low over the waves, away from the ship.

"The hull will start burning in no time!" exclaimed Sir Bastion, rather awed by what he had done.

"Whew, what a smell," said Sir Tenley, holding his nose.

"Singing makes a man dry," Jacques lurched over to the barrel and tipped it up, but no wine came out. "Crénom de Dieu – you've drunk the lot. There isn't a drop left."

The sailors became suddenly quiet; one had to be careful with Jacques when his temper turned sour.

Jacques picked up the barrel in a fury, stood it on end and gave it a resounding blow with his huge clenched fist. The round wooden top fell inside with a hollow clatter. "Time to throw the girl over the side," he bellowed, looking for something else to destroy. Before Myste had time to scream, he had unlocked the fetter round her ankle, tossed her over his shoulder and was striding towards the ship's side.

"Don't throw her away – she's mine! I'm taking her to France!" cried Pierre About, tackling his knees and spoiling his balance.

"Notsofast – hic – shesmine," Pierre the cook, a fat man, had pinned down both his feet.

As Jacques fell, he threw Myste into the arms of Pierre Squinteyes who wasn't expecting her. Knocking him over, she sent him rolling all the way down the tilting deck.

"You've broken my crumhorn . . . scrogeuneus . . . you've broken my crumhorn." Nearly in tears, he searched for the pieces in the dark.

Jacques, up on his feet again, was likewise searching for Myste.

"What's that bright light over there?" The minstrel pointed to the ominous glow reflected by the waves.

"Fire," yelled Jacques, suddenly sober. "The ship's a-fire!"

"She's – hic – burning by the stern."

"She's – hic – sterning by the burn."

From now on, everything happened very quickly. The sailors chased each other along the deck, running over Sir Vere de Pression just as he had got to sleep, and sweeping

124

him with them as they scrambled up the rope ladder to the aftercastle, treading on each other's fingers. Then they all leaned over to see what was happening below: they saw the smoke, but the blaze was hidden by the boards of the deck. Their combined weight caused *Le Pourquoi Pas?* to rise at the bows and sink at the stern, forcing the "fireship" under water. There was a terrifying hiss followed by a shower of scalding steam which sent the men scurrying back faster than they had come; but when the steam disappeared, Sir Vere de Pression had gone with it. Dazed and dreaming, he had hung over the ship's side, lost his bearings and plummeted overboard.

The ship righted herself when the weight returned to the centre, and water started to pour steadily through a gaping black hole that had been burnt in the hull. And then it rained. The clouds simply ripped their sides and poured water into the wind. It came down in torrents.

"There they are – the murderers! Those are the men who fired our ship." Jacques wrung water out of his beard with one hand and pointed to the long-boat, poised on top of a wave, with the other.

The shout was heard by Sir Tenley and put him off his stroke. He missed the sea, pulled on air and turned a neat somersault into the bottom of the boat.

"Load the catapult," screamed Jacques. "Fetch the cross-bows."

The men rushed back to the aftercastle in a tight jostling crowd and the ship tilted again.

For a moment, Myste and Sir Lute found themselves alone in the sloping bows.

"Quick. This is our chance to reach the long-boat," he said.

Myste had never dared to speak to Sir Lute before because she was too shy, and now she was too frightened. "H-how?" was all she managed to stutter, pointing to the

125

raging sea.

He looked completely at a loss. "Between me and God, there must be some way of crossing the water."

Paralysed, they watched a stone leave the catapult with an unsteady jerk, soar through the air and splash into the sea – missing the long-boat by a good furlong. A wild shower of cross-bow bolts followed, landing all over the place. The boat edged in closer.

"What's to be done?" she cried, staring at it and biting her nails. "I can't swim."

"Neither can I," he replied, desperately trying to think of a plan and finding his mind empty. The ivory lute was getting wet, so he automatically stuffed it back in its bag.

As Jacques came pounding back along the deck, Myste clutched her skirts, ran to the empty wine cask and dived head first into it. Then she hid herself by pushing the wooden top back into its groove from underneath.

"Where's the woman?" demanded Jacques, dagger in hand.

Sir Lute pointed up to the little castle on the mast and said nothing. He hated telling lies.

"Ha! Climbed the rigging, has she? Hoped to hide at the mast-head?" Jacques took three paces, swung himself into the ropes and started to climb.

Sir Lute rapped urgently on the top of the cask.

"Who is it?" came a tiny frightened whisper.

"Don't be alarmed – it's me." He pushed the wooden disc down, quickly wrapped the lute in the goatskin and handed the bundle to her. "Take this with you and hold it carefully – it's my dearest possession."

"But where am I going? Have you thought of a plan?"

"I'm going to float you across to the long-boat."

"In the barrel!"

"Between me and God, I wouldn't do such a thing if there was any other way."

126

Sir Lute rolled the barrel on to its side and Myste pushed the top back into place. She was sealed up as tight as a cask of salt herrings. Finding a length of rope, Sir Lute bound the barrel round and about and then realized it was too heavy to lift over the bulwark.

Jacques, having got to the mast head and found himself cheated, was venting his fury by dropping stones on the long-boat. It was so close, it would have been an easy target if the waves would only stop flinging it about. Having run out of stones, he decided to murder the minstrel who had tricked him; he looked down and noticed the hatchway was open.

Sir Lute had used the axe – left lying on deck – to wrench away the ladder leading below. He was setting it up between the hatchway and the bulwark to form a ramp.

Following the word "traitor" with a terrible oath, Jacques leapt for a rope and slid all the way down to the

steeply-sloping deck. He landed just as Sir Lute was rolling the barrel up the ladder.

"I'll carve you in pieces!" roared Jacques, picking up his axe.

Sir Lute turned. There was a sudden tempestuous gust of wind. The ship lurched sickeningly towards the sea. The barrel rolled gravely up the ramp, stopped, rolled forward again, teetered on the edge, then gently toppled into empty space.

"Catch!" Sir Lute yelled to Sir Bastion.

The timing could not have been worse. A wave – the size of a small mountain – came surging along the sea. It swept the long-boat to one side of it and the barrel landed on the other. There was a high foaming ridge of water in between.

"Myste – Myste –" cried Sir Bastion making a grab at the barrel as it re-appeared, dancing up to his fingers, then swirled out of his reach. "Row for dear life," he yelled at Sir Tenley as they chased the round bobbing shape that rolled into the troughs of waves, spun round in the spray, and sometimes got lost behind a sheet of rain.

Aboard *Le Pourquoi Pas?*, Sir Lute was too busy avoiding the axe to see what had happened.

"You should have kept the wine inside the barrel," he shouted to Jacques as he ducked, pulled off his hood and threw the flapping wet garment in the face of his opponent.

"The ship's sinking," chorused the crew, trying to bail out the water that had flooded the hold.

"The ladder's gone. The stern deck's a-wash, so we're trapped," came the despairing voice of Pierre Below.

Jacques flung the hood aside. "By Lucifer, if we're to go to Hell, I'll split your skull and take you with us." He raised his axe, rushed forward and met the minstrel's gown, rolled into a ball, bang between the eyes. He reeled, forgot where he was, tripped and fell through the open hatchway, landing on the rest of the crew with a splash.

The sea was nearer than it had been before. Sir Lute, now stripped to his underwear, carefully tucked his shirt into his braies, picked up the ladder and stepped into the surging water.

Some distance away, the long-boat was turning in mad circles, up and down on the waves.

"What are you doing – idiot – row *forward*," Sir Bastion cried in a frenzy of anguish.

"Must wait for Sir Lute, you know. Can't leave him to drown," Sir Tenley was doing his best to row the other way.

"We can't abandon her . . . alone in that barrel. If you don't help to catch it . . . I'll never forgive you . . . as long as I live."

The words were lost in the wind.

"We won't . . . any of us . . . live long in this tempest." Sir Tenley pointed to yet another wave hanging cliff-like above their heads.

Sir Lute, still clinging to the wooden ladder, was being swept along by the wave. When it broke, it seemed to fling him at the long-boat quite deliberately.

"Sweet Jesus," gasped Sir Lute, spitting out salt water as they helped him aboard. "I thought I should have drowned. Where's Myste?"

No one spoke. The long-boat tossed and turned with each fresh gust of wind.

"Only a miracle can save her now," murmured Sir Lute as he crossed himself.

Through the waves, they watched the French ship go down.

XI

HOW MYSTE GOT A
FIT OF THE GIGGLES AND
HOW SIR LUTE ENDED
HIS QUEST

The three men in the long-boat spent the rest of the night
rowing up and down the stormy sea, searching for Myste.
Barrel-like shapes played hide and seek in the waves, but
always turned out to be shadows cast by the moon. Later,
they saw drifting timbers from *Le Pourquoi Pas?* but that
was all.

The first glimmer of light shone on a hopeless empty sea.
The wind had died and the water rose and fell under a chill
white mist.

"We'll never find her now, she must surely be drowned."
Sir Lute's face was grey with cold and his teeth were
chattering. He stood up and re-wrapped the cloak he had
borrowed from Sir Bastion tightly round his shoulders.
He was a tall man and it left his legs colder than ever.

"It was my fault. I should have thrown myself into the
water and clung to the ropes round the barrel. I might have
been able to do something to save her. At least I should
have died with her and she wouldn't have been alone."
Shivering without his cloak, Sir Bastion stared miserably
at the bottom of the boat.

"No," said Sir Lute. "It was a stupid plan. I should
have thought of a better one."

Sir Tenley stopped rowing and carefully inspected his blistered hands. "By me troth, what does it matter whose fault it is? She's dead isn't she? So it's no good looking further."

He slowly turned the bows of the long-boat and rowed for the shore. The grey shape of a high cliff floated towards them. It was a ragged cliff, broken up like an old cheese. The water below was full of boulders.

Sir Tenley chatted to warm up their spirits, but it made his silent companions more wretched than ever. "I say, looking over my shoulder all night's given me a crick in the neck. It's stuck, I swear. I don't fancy the idea of spending the rest of my life with my head on back to front. Stupid things, boats. I wouldn't ride a horse backwards." He got up clumsily and sat the other way. "That's better," he said rubbing his neck. "Hey, what's that over there?"

"It's a rock," said Sir Lute severely.

"I know it's a rock, but why is it moving?"

The faster they rowed towards the shore, the more barrel-like the moving rock became. It was gently bobbing about in a deep pool, cut off from the sea by a ridge of pebbles. The rope still bound it round and about.

"It's a miracle – you said she'd be saved by a miracle!" cried Sir Tenley. "Or else the barrel was swept in by the storm and left stranded when the tide went out. Perhaps it's been lying there most of the night."

The three men scrambled into the surf and hastily beached the long-boat. Then they hauled the barrel out of the pool and up the dry pebbly slope.

"You open it. I haven't the courage," said Sir Lute.

Using his dagger to cut the cord, Sir Bastion gently eased the wooden circle out of its groove, turned it sideways and pushed it in. The barrel sloped towards the sea and Myste seemed to slide out like a slippery mermaid. A scarlet mermaid. She looked as if she'd been dipped in a

131

vat of scarlet dye. Her skin, hair, feet and gown were all the same appalling colour.

"Blood?" whispered Sir Tenley hoarsely.

"It's the wrong colour for blood." Sir Lute gazed sadly at Myste. He picked up the leather bag and drew out his ivory lute – now pink in patches – to see if it was broken.

"She's breathing!" cried Sir Bastion joyfully. "She's alive!"

Myste opened her eyes, sat up, gave a semi-circular smile, greeted them with a vague wave of the hand, stared out to sea and started to giggle.

"She's lost her mind," said Sir Tenley in a hollow voice.

Sir Lute, who had been watching Myste attentively, suddenly broke into a chuckle. This made her giggle more and in a few seconds she was wild with mirth. Pointing at her, he clutched his side, collapsed on the pebbles, leant against a rock and began to roar with laughter. He was so amused, he could hardly speak for over a minute.

"It's not funny," yelled Sir Bastion, furious.

"She's not mad," explained Sir Lute between bursts of merriment. "She's drunk. Think of the fumes inside the barrel . . . look at the colour of the wine. That good

Burgundy's gone to her head."

At this moment, a young man came hurrying down the side of the cliff, shouting triumphantly and leaping from boulder to boulder. He stopped every so often to blow a resounding blast on his horn.

"That's my squire," cried Sir Tenley with an answering whoop of joy. "So the rest of the men can't be far away. They must have been searching the coast for us."

From now on everything went splendidly. The small company of servants who had set out with the knights when they left home the day before could be seen standing at the top of the cliff. There were plenty of willing hands to carry Myste to the nearest place of shelter. This turned out to be and old, blackened, tumbledown hall, with the smoke pouring out of the hole in the turf roof, and cows lowing and chickens scratching about inside the hall. The earth floor was full of holes and it smelt like a stable.

The man who owned this place was called Baron Moore, and he was poor but hospitable. He said the men were welcome to sit by his fire for as long as they liked and Myste would be well looked after by his daughter.

They stayed there for the whole of Sunday, attending Mass at a nearby chapel. They slept in the hall the following night.

Myste had got over the effects of the wine by Monday morning. Her clothes had been scrubbed clean, she was her own colour again and the party was ready to leave.

Having rescued her from the French, they next wondered what to do with her. Sir Bastion wanted to carry her off to Chasemwell Hall and marry her at once, but Sir Lute firmly declared that she must be returned to Sterlyng Castle where she belonged. He wanted to see Sir Taxe's face when he saw her again. He intended to ask some awkward questions, try to get at the truth and then see that

133

justice was done. So to Sterlyng Castle they went.

It was a long journey. Sir Tenley's squire lent Myste his horse and Sir Lute – wearing his own clothes and looking more distinguished than ever – trotted on one side of her while Sir Bastion rode on the other. Sir Tenley pranced ahead on Passemall and the little company of servants clattered along behind. Everyone felt carefree and gay. No one was in a hurry to arrive.

There was plenty of time to talk on the way. They told Myste all the things she had been bursting to know, but too shy to ask. How Sir Bastion had gone to the inn at the cross roads and bought the juggler's clothes – which Sir Lute complained were creeping with lice. How he had sold his best greyhound to raise enough money to buy the skiff from the ruined ship-building yard at Fishport. How they had hidden among the rocks on the high stone ridge; waited for Sir Taxe and his armed escort to come marching along the road and seen him turn round and go home again.

Sir Lute decided to keep his secret about Myste's parents. He would tell her gently, after he had spoken with Sir Taxe.

When they arrived at Great Sterlyng village, they found it deserted, which was strange because Monday was a work-day. There were no men harvesting in the fields and no men plying their trades beside their huts. Windows were shuttered and doors were barred.

And at Sterlyng Castle, the drawbridge was up and the white walls were forbidding and silent.

Sir Bastion yelled for the porter, but nobody came.

"Something's wrong," cried Myste, getting more and more nervous.

Riding uneasily round the outer bank of the moat, they halted at the east side of the castle and shouted again. After a long wait, something moved behind one of the windows and then finally a rounded shape climbed out on

the roof, holding its sides and puffing and panting fit to burst.

"By all them . . . Holy Saints!" Molly Coddlem looked down and nearly fell over the battlements at what she saw. "It's a ghost . . . the walking dead . . . no, Glory be to Heaven, it's little Myste what's come home safe and well. Wait while I summon help and wind down the bridge."

Molly Coddlem disappeared and some time later the main drawbridge came rattling down with a thump, bringing the portcullis up as it did so. Then she ran along the bridge to the outer gatehouse, closely followed by a ragged little kitchen lad. When the second drawbridge had been lowered, she stood panting in the gateway, heaving with emotion and smiling all over her face.

"The castle seems completely deserted," said Sir Lute as they rode over the bridge, Molly Coddlem puffing along beside him. "Where are Sir Taxe and the garrison?"

She stopped and threw up her hands. "What, haven't you heard the tidings? There's been shockin' carryings on – a disgrace – and at harvest time too."

The horses were walked through the stout gatehouse and into the courtyard.

"It's a crying shame . . . all yesterday they was hearing

Mass and sharpening their weapons. I don't call it Christian to pray in church and then talk of nothink but bloody murder."

"Stop chattering and tell us plainly what's happened," cried Sir Bastion, out of patience, as he helped Myste to slide down from her horse. Sir Tenley had already dismounted, tied Passemall to a ring in the wall and was releasing the girths.

Molly Coddlem looked put out, like a chicken with ruffled feathers. "If you want the plain truth: Sir Taxe has gone and mustered an army and he's left to make war on Sir Pressitt." She then gave a full account of the raid.

To Myste, life was getting more and more like a bad dream. "But why has everybody gone?" she asked, staring at the broken window of the ladies' bower. Apart from five or six serving girls and a few small pantry lads, the whole castle seemed to be empty.

"Well, take Lady Crippling for a start. She's been raging mad against Sir Pressitt and can't wait to get her claws into him. She'd wear armour and wield a sword like a man if they'd let her. Wild horses wouldn't keep a woman like her at home."

"I can't imagine Lady Super and Lady Ida Dora in a military camp."

Molly Coddlem gave a contemptuous snort. "They've left with more noise than good sense, if you ask me. They can't abide living in tents; but they'll not stay here a single day wi'out soldiers to protect them."

"Aren't there any men here at all – not even a porter?" inquired Sir Bastion.

"Peter Doubt the porter's here; but he's like to die on account of the thumping great clout dealt him by Sir Pressitt."

"Who's that over there?"

Sir Bastion was pointing to a blind serf with a nasty cut

136

on his forehead who had come out of the kitchen and was groping his way round the courtyard; one hand holding a wooden bowl, the other feeling the wall.

Molly Coddlem shrugged her huge shoulders. "He's of no odds, being blind. He's only taking food to the prisoner."

Sir Lute was instantly alert. "What prisoner?"

"Why, the dangerous madman they keep out of harm's way under the turret. He's always been there – leastwise as long as I can remember."

'I think I'll take a look at this madman."

"But you can't," cried Myste, "he's possessed of the Devil!"

The blind man disappeared through the large stable door and – although Myste and Molly Coddlem tried hard to stop him – Sir Lute softly followed. He was led past the empty stalls to a door set in the angle of the wall. Beyond this was a store room; a dark six–sided place, lit by arrow loops and smelling of hay. Immediately to the right, half lost in the shadows, was a door about four feet high.

The blind man fumbled among the tangle of objects hanging on leather thongs from his belt. He found a key, fitted it to the lock, turned it and swung the door open. The stair beyond dived down, steep as a rabbit burrow. There was a dwarf size door at the bottom: bolted, not locked.

"I'll carry the prisoner's food myself."

The voice sounded hollow, unearthly, in that stone passage. Thinking it was a spirit from another world, the blind man dropped the bowl and started to scuttle back up the stairs.

"Hold." The knight caught him by the arm. "I'll have the key before you go – otherwise I might find myself locked in as well."

Having cut the key off with his dagger, Sir Lute watched the blind man creep to the top of the stairs. Then he turned and unbolted the door.

He immediately felt as if he had stepped into the bottom of a disused well. A dirty well. It stank of drains, damp and old straw. It was hard to breathe in such thick air. The prison being far below the level of the moat, the only ventilation came from two shafts slanting upwards at the very top of the circular wall. Water pattered on to the stone floor which was alive with slithering plopping noises.

"Mind the frogs as you put down the bowl . . . sniff . . . they've got longer to live than I have."

The cell looked absolutely empty. All Sir Lute could see in the dim light was a huge pile of rotting straw and the voice seemed to come from the middle of it. Frogs of all sizes crept over the floor; it was swarming with them.

"This fever'll be the death of me, but it's better to be buried dead than buried alive." It sounded as if one of the frogs was speaking, the words came in such a croaking whisper. "Take care, or you'll squash King Henry . . . he's squatting under your left shoe."

Sir Lute edged forward, avoiding the frogs by feeling the flagstones with his feet. The straw gave an agitated rustle, heaved, and flung itself apart, revealing the old prisoner – who had been lying in the centre to keep out the cold – sitting bolt upright with straw sticking out of his rags like the stuffing coming out of a scarecrow.

"Who are you?" demanded Sir Tiff Fide, his eyes starting out of his head with terror.

Sir Lute recognized the strange shape of Sir Tiff Fide's nose. He remembered his bushy eyebrows. Apart from the wild tangle of hair, that had grown, all the rest of the stout warrior had shrunk to skin and bone. He looked so frail and ill, Sir Lute decided to be careful how he broke the news.

"I'm an old friend."

"The Devil you're not. The only friends I have left to me are these frogs." He indicated them with a sweep of his

138

hand. "I command whole armies of them: kings, earls, knights and squires. As it happens, you're standing on Eleanor of Aquitaine. She's encamped with her husband and you've caught her by the flipper."

Sir Lute raised his foot and let the frog jump away. "I've come to set you free."

The prisoner got very agitated. "Ha. So that's your way of putting it. Now I know who you are. Been expecting you for years. Can't scare an old warrior like me with your black beard and dagger. Snuffed out like a candle, is it? Re-lit in another world?"

Puzzled, Sir Lute bent down to give Sir Tiff Fide a closer look at his face, but the old man recoiled into the straw as if he had been bitten by a snake.

"He can't remember me," Sir Lute whispered to Sir Bastion and Sir Tenley who had dared to follow him down the stairs.

"Ha. Three assassins, are there? Three men sent to

finish me off," insisted Sir Tiff Fide, rattling his chains.

"You must have changed a lot since he last saw you," whispered Sir Bastion.

Sir Lute rubbed his chin. "My beard, of course. I didn't have one in those days."

"Why don't you describe his horse," suggested Sir Tenley.

"Remember your grey charger? His name was Wyde-Gyrth."

"Yes, yes . . . sniff . . . my old charger. Blown out with feeding . . . round as a barrel. Wyde-Gyrth."

"Try his sword," said Sir Bastion.

"You called your sword Slyce-em."

Very upset, the old man tugged his beard as if he wanted to tug it out and stared hard at his frogs. Taking a straw, he gave King Henry a sudden vicious prod and sent him leaping from puddle to puddle.

"How come you know my horse and sword?"

"Because I was your squire."

With a weird, strangled cry that sounded vaguely like "Gramercy," Sir Tiff Fide clutched his chains, fell back and hit his head a smacking great blow on the wet wall. He lay absolutely still, with his feet in the air and his eyes and mouth wide open.

"I've killed him," cried Sir Lute, calling loudly for a file from the armoury and a pitcher of wine.

All this time, Myste and Molly Coddlem had been left trembling in the courtyard and when Sir Bastion and Sir Tenley came rushing out of the stable door, they thought their worst suspicions about the prisoner were confirmed. Myste ran to the gatehouse, while Molly Coddlem fled to the pantry and locked herself in.

After an unbearable silence, Myste peeped out of the window and saw Sir Bastion on his way back to the stable with a file in his hand, colliding with Sir Tenley carrying a pitcher. She could not understand what was happening and, curiosity getting the better of her, crept into the stable to listen. She head a rasping sound from the prison below. Then, plucking up her courage, she went into the dark store room just as slow steps were coming up the stairs. The door opened and Sir Lute ducked under the archway and stepped into the narrow strip of light cast by the single arrow loop. He carried a heavy bundle that was stiff and grey, like a huge clay doll that had been given a beard.

"W-who is he?" whispered Myste.

"He is your grandfather, Sir Tiff Fide."

The shadows creeping round the courtyard at Sterlyng Castle told the time like a sundial. Several hours had passed. It was six o'clock.

Sir Bastion sat on the mounting block and watched Sir Lute stride up and down. Every so often they both looked towards the great chamber where Sir Tiff Fide lay sleeping – Myste in attendance.

A truckle bed had been wheeled from the ladies' bower into the empty space where Sir Taxe's bedstead used to stand. The old knight had been laid on it, carefully washed, wrapped in a sheet and covered with warm blankets. His rags had been thrown on the kitchen fire and burned with a terrible smell.

Myste, who was now convinced that the Bezoar was a solid lump of magic, had taken it from the bodice of her gown and hung it round her grandfather's neck. It had saved her from the storm, she declared, so it would most certainly cure him.

Sir Tiff Fide had come to himself slowly, asking where he was and what had he been doing to give himself such a terrible bump on the head. He seemed to have forgotten all about his long imprisonment with the frogs; but he was quite clear about everything else. He recognized Sir Lute and understood who Myste was. He was proud of her and clung to her like a child.

Myste had always been in a muddle about herself, not knowing who she was or where she came from. Discovering a grandfather and being told that her real name was Myste Tiff Fide, only made her more bewildered than ever. Needless to say, Sir Lute soon told her the whole history of her parents: he talked of her brave father, Sir Morte Tiff Fide and of her beautiful mother, Berengaria Uracca. By the time he had finished, all the muddle in Myste's mind had disappeared and her face was as glowing and happy as twenty candles all burning together. It was warming just to look at her.

Sir Lute turned the situation over in his mind and continued to pace up and down the courtyard, smiting the clenched fist of one hand against the palm of the other. He had been out of his element at sea, slow to find a plan of action; but now one scheme was chasing another and there were too many of them.

"When Sir Taxe gets wind of what's happened, he'll march his entire army back here, re-take the castle and murder us all – Myste and Sir Tiff Fide first. We must defend ourselves."

"I'll send word to my father," broke in Sir Bastion, "he must come at once, bringing men and weapons. This castle's got the best modern defences I know of, well stocked with provisions. It can withstand a siege."

"Excellent; but we must arm ourselves against Sir Taxe in the king's name." Sir Lute was always on the side of law and order. "Our best defence would be to summon the sheriff."

"We can't put our trust in Sir Parr Stitt!" cried Sir Bastion, aghast. "Not only is he in his dotage, but he is utterly corrupt as well. He'll alter the law to suit himself. He's never refused a bribe in his life, which explains why he's so rich."

"I'll lodge a complaint about him as soon as I reach London," said Sir Lute firmly. "He's obviously unfit for the office; but a sheriff represents the king and we're safe once he's here. If we're lucky, he'll bring an efficient bailiff and a strong force of men. Sir Taxe would never dare attack Sir Parr Stitt – it would be open revolt against the state. We must send for him at once."

The shadows of the courtyard had got darker and colder. "A horse would have to gallop like the wind to reach the sheriff before dark," said Sir Bastion.

"Passemall can do it!" came a sudden whooping cry, which woke Sir Tiff Fide and brought Myste running to the window. Sir Tenley, almost bursting with excitement, had been standing in the doorway of the great hall, listening to the conversation.

The splendid horse was still bridled and saddled, tethered to the ring in the wall. Sir Bastion untied the reins while Sir Tenley took a running jump. The saddle swung round and deposited him on the stone cobbles the other side.

"More haste, less speed," said Sir Bastion, tightening the girths.

Having given the back of his tunic a good rub to make sure no bones were broken, Sir Tenley re-mounted. With a farewell flourish of the hand, he thundered through the gatehouse and away over the bridge. For the first time, he was urging Passemall forward instead of pulling him back.

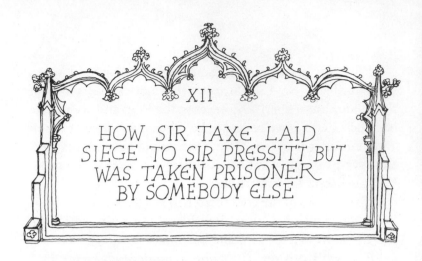

XII

HOW SIR TAXE LAID SIEGE TO SIR PRESSITT BUT WAS TAKEN PRISONER BY SOMEBODY ELSE

It had taken Sir Taxe all day to march his huge unruly army through the forest. Fully armed, mounted on his great war horse, he raged against Sir Pressitt as he went along. At noon he had called for a halt and whipped up the spirits of his men to a state of murderous excitement by delivering a speech that would have done credit to Julius Caesar. No one had ever liked Sir Pressitt anyway, and by the time they came out of the forest and saw him standing on the top turret of his keep, each man drew his weapon and ran forward with a blood-curdling yell. The only trouble was that the grey flagstone walls of Castle Skint got in the way. Sir Pressitt and the bedstead were inside; Sir Taxe was outside; and the drawbridge was up.

The frustrated army rampaged about all three sides of the castle, and Sir Taxe's merchant ships – which had already started their voyage up the river – were to blockade the water side. All Sir Taxe could do was yell abuse at Sir Pressitt and post sentries to stop supplies getting through. This did not suit the army, who had sharpened their weapons to do battle, not to go bird watching.

Sir Taxe pitched his camp at the edge of a little wood on rising ground to the south of the castle. It was arranged like

a village with a large highly-decorated tent, to be used as a
church, in the centre, the richly-embroidered pavilions of
Sir Taxe's household beside it, and the grubby canvas
tents, improvised shelters of interwoven branches, and
holes in the ground covered with bracken, belonged to the
common soldiers, and sprawled over the hillside like untidy
slums.

There was a bit of a frost that first night. The moon
sparkled on the gilded ram that pranced on top of Sir Taxe's
large eight-sided pavilion. He lay shivering inside, too cold
to get to sleep, twisting and turning on a scratchy straw
palliasse that was rustling with insects. Then he pictured
Sir Pressitt lying snug and warm in his own deep feather
mattress and he had soon worked himself up into such a
passion – it was as good as an extra blanket.

The moon had no difficulty in scaling walls and getting
into castles. It inspected every cracked stone of Castle
Skint, and showed them up clear as daylight – only in
black and white.

Castle Skint had been built by Henry I in 1130 and no
one had repaired or altered it since. The curtain wall
encircled the bailey as stoutly as ever, but the buildings
inside were decayed and some of them – like the old hall –
had tumbled down altogether. As Sir Pressitt couldn't

afford to re-build it, he lived in the great, square, crumbling keep and established his hall on the second storey. Apart from the thick layers of rushes on the floor, which hadn't been changed for twenty years, the room looked like the inside of a cathedral. The walls were over thirty feet high; pierced by arrow loops at the bottom and lit by a series of fine round-headed arches at the level of a gallery that ran through the thickness of the outer wall at the top. An arcade divided the room into equal halves, with Sir Pressitt sleeping on one side, and his men laid out in rows like a catch of fish, at the other. The arches were decorated by the barbaric zig-zag ornament so dear to Norman masons, which always vaguely reminded Sir Pressitt of knitting.

The stolen bedstead had been set up in Sir Pressitt's part of the room, beyond the arcade. It appeared more shrine-like than ever, standing behind the massive pillars. It looked superb.

Despite his vivid imagination, Sir Taxe hadn't done justice to Sir Pressitt's sublime contentment. He had answered insult with insult and got his revenge. He was satisfied. He dropped off to sleep with a happy smile on his

ugly face and dreamed of Sir Taxe resting on a hard camp
bed. He overslept and got up reluctantly. He ate his breakfast and then lingered at the board of his long greasy table,
rolling little bits of bread into pellets and watching Willy
Doolittle beyond the arcade, as he shook out the huge
embroidered mattress he had been lying on.

The servants had stacked their straw palliasses against
the wall and set up trestle tables. They always took their
meals in the hall, together with their lord. The room was
crowded, for Sir Pressitt had called in about fifty of his
liege men to defend the castle.

"Have you ever clapt eyes on such carving?" Hugh
Woods jerked his elbow in his neighbour's ribs and pointed
his knife at the bedstead. Being a carpenter, he appreciated
good craftsmanship.

"There's jewels in that headboard, and gold and silver,"
old Hammer Smith told anyone who cared to listen.

Willy Doolittle gave an enormous sneeze as he laid the
mattress on the bedstead and flattened it with a rod. A
feather had gone up his nose.

"Sir Taxe be in a mighty hurry to get this back," he
grinned.

"Sir Taxe can stamp and shout as much as he likes, it only
serves to make me laugh," boasted Sir Pressitt, leaving the
table and swaggering about in front of his men. "Mere
threats can't hurt us."

Ivor Grudge, who had been scowling at the enemy from
one of the large gallery windows, overheard this remark,
swung round and yelled down at the hall. "You're mistaken,
he means more than threats. He intends a deal o' business."

"It'll take a better man than Sir Taxe to batter his way
into this castle," said Sir Pressitt, still bragging.

He had reason to be confident, for there were few strong-
holds in the whole of England as impregnable as Castle
Skint. Superbly sited on solid rock, it had a sheer drop

down to the river, and there was a deep ditch on the land-ward sides. There was a stout gatehouse, a water-gate and three square towers to defend the curtain wall. Added to which, the masonry at the base of the keep was over twelve feet thick. No one could force a way into that great stone box.

"Looks like he's going to make some war machines. He's brought enough gear wi' him," Grudge yelled down again.

Sir Pressitt stopped boasting and strode over the springy rushes, up the dark stairway and joined Grudge in the gallery. He looked through the window and saw about eight waggons drawn up at the edge of the forest. Sir Taxe's carpenters were busily unloading huge pieces of wood, ropes, nets and winches. It was a formidable sight.

"By all the fiends in Hell! He can't batter our castle with war machines!" exclaimed Sir Pressitt indignantly. "Castle Sking belongs to the king. Why – it's against the law."

This was true. Henry I had given the castle to one of his barons – Josse de Pressitt – to command and for his heirs for ever; Sir Pressitt was the last of these heirs.

"King Edward's a doddery old man now, he don't keep strong rule any more," argued Grudge. "Seems we'll have to look to our own defence."

Sir Pressitt ruffled his moustache until it stuck out like a scrubbing brush. "Then we must make some machines of our own."

"Come to think on it, there's several stowed away at the back of the smithy. They're old and broken, but there's a couple as could be mended."

Sir Pressitt thoughtfully returned to the hall. "We're safe enough here," he told his men. "This castle has stood for well over two hundred years; it's been attacked several times, but never taken. That mealy-mouthed merchant can't harm us." Saying this, he banged his fist fiercely against the wall and brought down a huge lump of crumbling plaster.

Throughout the rest of that day and the next, Sir Pressitt kept careful watch on Sir Taxe's army, and Sir Taxe did his best to catch sight of Sir Pressitt's men as they crouched behind the battlements. They exchanged arrows and a great deal of bad language; but apart from that, nothing happened.

By Wednesday morning, Sir Taxe – still blissfully ignorant of the goings-on at home – found he was having trouble with his army. It was made up of trained companies of men from his villages. (Owing to the threat of French invasion, every man between the ages of fifteen and fifty had been given a weapon and taught how to use it.) These serfs and peasant farmers were angry at being dragged away from their fields at harvest time when the weather was so splendid. They wanted to murder Sir Pressitt, re-capture the bedstead, and get home before it started to rain. Bored and frustrated, they started picking quarrels and scrapping among themselves, fighting each other with knives, axes and war hammers.

Egged on by his mother, Sir Taxe moved among his unruly troops and tried to placate them. Sir Charge marched to his right, and Hugo First followed a step behind.

"Patience. How can we get to grips with the enemy until we have constructed our war machines?" Sir Taxe demanded, pointing to a group of serfs who had chopped down some tall trees and were busy trimming off the branches for the main beams of the giant trebuchet they were going to make. This was to be a huge counterweighted sling for throwing stones into the castle. Other carpenters were sawing and shaping the smaller tree trunks needed for ordinary trebuchets. "We're not birds, we can't fly over the walls," continued Sir Taxe, "we have to batter our way through them; and to do that, we must make a battering ram."

The men kept a sulky silence, so Sir Taxe started off again.

"Of course, the best way to get into the castle would have been to undermine one of the towers, and that's what we've been trying to do." He waved an arm at a group of dirty, surly, rebellious serfs armed with picks and mattocks. "These hard-working, uncomplaining miners have been trying to dig a tunnel, but it appears that the castle's built on rock . . ."

The soldiers did not listen, they just watched Sir Taxe's mouth opening and shutting under his drooping grey moustache. It was the only part of him that they could see, all the rest being hidden by armour of one sort or another. He still wore the coat of plates under the splendid ram-embroidered cloth jupon, widely laced to allow for his stoutness; but he had done away with the closed helm he had used at the combat. He said it gave him a feeling of claustrophobia and had replaced it with a kettle hat. The deep crown and wide brim completely covered the top half of his head.

". . . we had been hoping to undermine that turret over there." Sir Taxe was still talking, rather spinning it out. He pointed up at one of the corner turrets of the keep and caught sight of Sir Pressitt gingerly trying his weight on the old wooden gallery, or hoarding, that jutted out all round the top at battlement level. He wore a dirty plum-coloured surcoat, cut short in the front, over cloth-covered iron plates that were scalloped at the edges; and beneath that hung a triangular shape that was the bottom of a shirt of mail. An enormous two-handed sword hung by his side.

Sir Taxe stopped in mid-speech, walked to within bowshot of the wall and shook both fists at Sir Pressitt. "Robber," he cried, "foul, stinking varlet. Open your gates and give me back my bedstead."

"I defy you," yelled Sir Pressitt, leaning on the rickety timber and then quickly stepping back when he realized it would not support him. "I've taken your bedstead as a token of my revenge. Now that I've got it, I'll defend it with my life. Why don't you go home, and take your farmyard rabble with you?"

"Lower your drawbridge, come out and fight like a man. You're afraid to face me, chicken-hearted churl."

"If my heart's like a chicken's, then you've no more guts than a mouse. If you want your bedstead – come in and get it."

"You say that because you feel secure behind those stout walls; but you forget they make you a prisoner. You're locked up, like a bear in a cage. A bear can't fight when he's starving."

Sir Pressitt had no answer for this. Sir Taxe had acted so promptly, it had not allowed enough time for him to fill his bailey with animals, or his store rooms with supplies. He had to resort to rather pointless abuse. "You roar like a lion and act like a rabbit."

"You've got less sense than an earthworm and bray like an ass."

Sir Taxe, having shouted himself hoarse, turned his back on Sir Pressitt and returned to his camp. He felt depressed, harassed on all sides. Sir Pressitt seemed more cocksure than ever, and he wondered why.

In the camp, the cooks were busy preparing the mid-day meal. Several geese were being roasted on a very long spit over a wood fire; pots and cauldrons were steaming and simmering in the ashes. The smell of food wafted happily through the air. Sir Taxe retired to his pavilion to rest.

With a sigh of relief, he took off his heavy iron hat and sat on the straw bed. He was just about to lie back and put his feet up when something landed outside with a frightful earth-shaking thud. Sir Taxe sat bolt upright and hurriedly put his hat back on his head. The screams and groans coming from the outside sounded like a massacre.

"The dinner is ruined!" cried Lady Super Taxe, running in, hotly pursued by her pack of dogs. "A great stone fell on it."

"Hazard of war," said Sir Taxe, striding towards the entrance to his pavilion and bumping into Lady Ida Dora Mann. He wished with all his heart that the women had stayed in their proper place – Sterlyng Castle.

"The geese are all burnt and the sauces are full of cinders," Lady Ida Dora cried dismally.

"There must be something left to eat," said Sir Taxe, trying to move away, but his wife had clutched hold of his gauntlet.

"My pavilion is full of ants," she complained, "they're crawling all over my silk chemises . . ."

"And a field mouse nested in my new head-dress," interrupted Lady Ida Dora. "It's eaten one of the pearls."

"This is a military camp, not a royal palace," said Sir Taxe with dignity.

Hugo First came in to report that the enemy had mounted a catapult on top of a tower and the whole camp would have to be moved further back if they did not want it to be wrecked with stones.

Sir Taxe escaped from his pavilion and went to view the damage. He found the cooks grouped disconsolately round the ruin of their fire, raking the blackened bodies of the geese out of the scattered ashes. A large corner stone – torn from one of the ruined buildings in the bailey – had landed on top of the spit and bent it. Over on the mural tower, Sir Taxe could just see the arm of the catapult being

winched down ready for re-loading, so he turned to study
its line of fire. He found himself staring at a company of
about a hundred men, marching towards him through the
scrubby bushes that grew at the edge of the forest. The
nearer they came, the more their livery looked like the
sheriff's livery; and the stout man at their head looked
remarkably like the sheriff's bailiff.

Sir Taxe had almost forgotten that he was attacking one
of the king's castles, now he remembered it. He wished
Sir Parr Stitt had come in person instead of sending his
bailiff. It was always difficult, offering a bribe through a
messenger.

Back at the castle, the stone left the catapult, flew in a
high arc and then came thudding down bang in the middle
of a puddle, just where the sheriff's bailiff was about to
put his foot. It splattered him all over with mud and
spoilt his dignity. He hastily retreated and stationed his
men at a safe distance beneath some trees.

Sir Taxe settled his kettle hat firmly on his head and
prepared for a difficult interview. His troops gathered
round to hear what the sheriff's bailiff had to say. He could
hear the yapping of the dogs, as Lady Super and Lady
Ida Dora left the pavilion and hurried towards them. Old

153

Lady Crippling came hobbling up over the grass as fast as she could, using two feet and a stick.

"God prosper you," Sir Taxe started off politely.

"I can't say I return your greeting," said the bailiff in a loud fruity voice.

"What greeting?" Sir Taxe was rather taken aback.

"About prospering. I've come to arrest you." The bailiff took a deep breath. "You are summoned to appear before the sheriff at Sterlyng Castle and answer to the charge of having laid hands on your elder brother the knight Sir Tiff Fide, rightful owner of the said castle, cast him into prison and confined him there for a period of fifteen years."

Sir Taxe looked as if the bailiff had given him a hard blow with a heavy axe. His legs failed, and he sat down suddenly on a fallen tree. His armour had a collapsed look about it, as if there was no one inside it.

Lady Crippling hobbled up to the bailiff and poked him with her stick.

"Adam's bones. Say that again."

The bailiff repeated the charge and followed it up with a detailed account of how Sir Tiff Fide had been discovered and released from his prison by Sir Lute, who had once been his squire.

No one believed this extraordinary story until they looked at Sir Taxe; large tears were trickling down his nose and dripping from the corners of his moustache. "I am undone," he muttered. "I'm completely ruined."

"Sir Lute is a base wretch, meddling in our affairs!" screamed Lady Super, flinging herself into the arms of her friend. "He's a low worthless fellow," comforted Lady Ida Dora, "what right had he to pry into the prison? He's hateful – I've entirely altered my opinion of him."

"He's earned a great reputation for valour," said the bailiff, trying to make himself heard above the general hubbub. "Assisted by the knights Sir Bastion and Sir

Tenley Knotte, he rescued the Maid Myste from the French. He says she is the knight Sir Tiff Fide's grandchild, and can prove it."

There was a fresh outburst of astonishment and Sir Taxe clutched his head and let out a great groan.

All this time, Lady Crippling had been jerking about, waving her stick and clawing at her wimple which seemed to have worked its way up over her mouth. Her veil had slipped sideways and her head was so tied up in a knot of white draperies that it looked as if she would either suffocate or strangle herself. Lady Ida Dora hastily disentangled her, whereupon the old woman dropped her stick, snatched up a handy sword and brandished it in the air. "Shame," she cried, standing over Sir Taxe with the air of an elderly avenging angel, "you've brought shame to yourself and your family."

"What else could I do?" sobbed Sir Taxe. "He'd come back to claim his estates."

"You told me that the man in the prison was a raving lunatic."

"So he is," muttered Sir Taxe.

"You said Myste was a foundling, when all the time you knew her to be your own kith and kin. Miserable man, you've been living in a dung heap of wickedness and deceit."

"Tell me what knight hasn't a secret or two hidden away underground," said Sir Taxe.

The catapult on the turret released another huge piece of masonry. Everyone turned and watched it soar up into the sky, then it dropped down to flatten a small tent.

"Sir Taxe must come and answer the charge at Sterlyng Castle," the bailiff repeated for the third time.

"I won't go," he cried through his tears, and he meant it.

The sheriff's officer looked at the large army spread out

155

before him and compared it to his own company of men. He decided to be prudent. The law was one thing, enforcing it another.

"I will deliver your answer to Sir Parr Stitt," he said.

Lady Crippling stumped forward and stuck the point of the sword firmly in the ground.

"I'd rather see my son hanged than called a coward," she cried furiously. "He'll behave with honour and answer the summons."

Old Lady Crippling was a remarkable woman: tough as an old boot, indomitable, not to be defeated under any circumstances. When all her family seemed to have lost their heads, she kept her own firmly attached to her ancient shoulders and took control of everything.

She gave Sir Charge command of the army and told him to press on with the siege. She then sent squires and grooms scurrying in all directions, falling over each other in their hurry to prepare the horses for the journey back to Sterlyng Castle. She had soon clambered into her horse litter; Lady Super wept dismally as she mounted her palfrey, while Lady Ida Dora did likewise with a long solemn face but such bright eyes that she was obviously enjoying every detail of this splendid scandal. Father Off accompanied the two ladies on his obstinate mule. The sheriff's bailiff, looking more pompous than ever, hauled himself into the saddle and watched Sir Taxe closely in case he should make a sudden dash for freedom.

Sir Taxe never thought of escape. He sat his horse limply with his head hanging down, refusing to speak to anyone and concentrating on a strange inner numbness which somehow deadened the pain of his humiliation.

His face had gone small and white under the round kettle hat, like the shrunken kernel of a walnut rattling about in its shell.

Before the nimblest young squire had recovered his breath, the whole clumsy cavalcade was travelling through the forest at a fast trot; the sheriff's men panting along behind, trying to keep up as best they could. They arrived at Sterlyng Castle just as the sun was going down.

The porter Peter Doubt had died, and one of the sheriff's servants stood in his place under the portcullis holding his jangling bunch of keys. The sheriff's bailiff ordered Sir Taxe to dismount and he was pushed up the dark narrow stairs to a room in the gatehouse that had a huge square lock on the door. The porter turned the key on Sir Taxe and a sentry was posted to guard him.

As soon as she saw her husband being dragged into the gatehouse, Lady Super let out a piercing scream, flung her gauze veil over her face and fled to the chapel, followed by a trail of lap-dogs and her faithful friend, Lady Ida Dora. Father Off gave heaven a despairing look, got down from his saddle and went to comfort them.

Having stepped heavily down from her litter and looked about her, Lady Crippling was disgusted to find her home swarming with Sir Prize's armed men. Hurrying through the main door of her hall, she found Sir Prize himself, sitting on a bench with Sir Cum Stance. They both looked at her sheepishly, waiting to see which way the wind was going to blow and hoping to veer about like a couple of weathercocks and blow along with it. Sir Parr Stitt was snoring in Sir Taxe's great chair with his feet on a footstool. Sir Bastion and Sir Tenley Knotte were together by the central hearth; but the man Lady Crippling wanted to see least of all wasn't there. She inquired about Sir Lute and was delighted to hear he had left the castle that very morning for London.

Sir Lute was a member of Prince Edward's household and his royal master had wanted to know where he was and why he hadn't arrived at Westminster. Messengers had been scouring the country for him and finally traced him to Sterlyng Castle. After a short conversation with them, he had ordered his servants to saddle his horse and galloped away in great haste.

Lady Crippling gave the knights in her hall a look of withering scorn and then slowly climbed the stairs to the great chamber.

She found Sir Tiff Fide propped against a mountain of cushions, his clean white hair spread round him like gossamer silk, his face about the same colour as his hair and his nose still red on account of his cold. His chest was wheezing like a pair of punctured bellows and he had to breathe through his mouth. Myste sat on a cushion by his bed, glad she was able to comfort her grandfather, but secretly wishing she was downstairs in the hall talking to Sir Bastion.

Old Lady Crippling stared down at her eldest son, searching the lines of his face for traces of the huge warrior who had set out for France all those years before.

Staring back, Sir Tiff Fide had the uncomfortable feeling that he had shrunk to being a little boy again. He recognized his mother at once and told himself to look out – she hadn't changed at all. He struggled to sit up, sneezed, fell back and waved a feeble hand at Myste.

"I'm not letting her out of my sight – sniff – not for a minute. It's not safe. Sir Taxe'll have her murdered if he can – or his wife will. Who's to protect her?"

"Her husband, of course."

"What husband?" Sir Tiff Fide sat up again and stared round the room as if the husband was hiding in one of the shadows.

"The husband we are going to find her. The sooner she is married, the better." The old lady dropped her stick and embraced Myste. Then the newly-discovered great-grand-mother stood back and inspected her critically, as if she'd never seen her before. "Here's good fortune!" she cried. "Her appearance is better than I thought. Dress her in silk, add a few jewels and I daresay she'll do us such credit that we can marry her to the richest knight in the shire."

"That's right," agreed Sir Tiff Fide. "A splendid warrior, someone who knows how to fight."

"Then you won't send me to a convent!" exclaimed Myste joyfully.

"Adam's bones, what nonsense. Remember you're a great heiress now – a fine lady. Only younger daughters of large families are given to the church. In your situation, you can choose any husband you like."

"Then I want to marry Sir Bastion," cried Myste, too excited to think carefully before speaking, then wishing she hadn't.

"Sir Prize's son!" screeched Lady Crippling.

"Nice boy; but not powerful enough," wheezed Sir Tiff Fide from his cushions. "The sort of champion I have in mind is a big burly man with muscles of iron."

Myste sat at the bedside, twisting her fingers together nervously while the other two glared at her as if she'd said something criminal.

"Not powerful enough!" echoed the old lady, dreadfully affronted. "He's not powerful at all! Sir Prize's lands are all mortgaged and his hall's as bare as a stable. You must choose from the great lords, men of authority and birth. Men with large possessions. We're not thinking of marrying you to a pauper."

Lady Crippling did not wait to hear Myste's timid but rebellious reply, and she stalked out of the room with her mouth set in a grim line. The line softened as she stumped down the curving stairs and by the time she reached the bottom it was turned up in a satisfied smile. She had thought of an ideal husband for Myste.

It was nearly supper time. Sir Parr Stitt was still snoring in the hall and the servants were setting up the tables noisily, as if he wasn't there. The other knights had left.

"Wake up my friend, we have business to discuss," Lady Crippling bellowed into the sheriff's ear.

"Eh . . . eh . . . what? Is it a raid?" he cried, alarmed and confused, while two squires lifted him to his gouty feet. Lady Crippling took him by the arm and led him down a couple of steps, across a damp store room that smelt of apples, to a door set in massive walls directly below Sir Taxe's oratory. It was a small thick door, studded with nails, decorated with huge curving hinges and secured by a great square lock. Lady Crippling fumbled among the folds of her gown and brought out an enormous key. She opened the door to reveal a little room that was filled with chests; they were piled one on top of the other right up to the vaulted ceiling: enamelled caskets, little silver-gilt shrines, gold candlesticks, and other priceless ornaments were scattered among them like odd pieces of cast-off rubbish. It was the castle treasury, or strong-room. The moment they were both inside, Lady Crippling turned and firmly locked the door.

"We can talk freely in this place. No one can hear us," she shouted.

Sir Parr Stitt had become suddenly wide awake and

161

there was a gleam in his watery old eyes as he looked at the
treasure. He was good at extracting bribes and – although
he was a bit hazy about the particulars of the case regarding
Sir Taxe and his brother – he felt he was about to clinch
the richest bargain of his career. He sat down on a gigantic
iron-bound oak chest and told himself that he would soon
own some of the goods inside it.

"Disgraceful business," he started off, speaking in
general terms because he didn't want to display his
ignorance. "Sir Taxe has behaved like a scoundrel and
shall hang for it."

"Sir Tiff Fide doesn't want to see his brother hanged,
for all the wrong he's done him!" exclaimed Lady Crippling. "Sir Tiff Fide has a noble, forgiving disposition, and
he'd never bring such shame to the rest of his own family."

"Sir Taxe will hang, for all that," said Sir Parr Stitt,
sticking to his point. "Or else have his head chopped off.
I'll see that justice is done – as a warning to others."

"Not if Sir Tiff Fide fails to bring a case against him."

Sir Parr Stitt pretended that he couldn't hear; and after

repeating the sentence twice, Lady Crippling knew she was wasting her breath so she came straight to the subject of her plan.

"Sir Tiff Fide has a grand-daughter who's young, obedient and in need of a husband," she said, walking round the room, tapping the chests with her stick. Then she opened the lid of one of them to show that it was brimful of gold and silver coins. Cupping her bony old hands together, she scooped up a heap of the little round discs and let them fall in a shower. "As there's no one else to inherit Sterlyng Castle, all this wealth will be hers."

Sir Parr Stitt, who had been a widower for many years, nodded his head and his eyes gleamed more brightly than ever. He knew what Lady Crippling was after: she was offering him Myste in marriage on the understanding that he should drop the charge against Sir Taxe. It did not take him long to come to a decision.

"Provided her dowry's good enough – I'll wed the girl myself."

"I knew you'd agree," shouted Lady Crippling, delighted at the success of her diplomacy.

"Sir Taxe had better retire to some small manor and live there quietly," said Sir Parr Stitt, with a twinge of conscience.

"We'll call in the lawyers tomorrow," cried Lady Crippling.

"Splendid, but you needn't shout so loud. Better keep this contract a secret for a week or two. Can't pardon Sir Taxe one day and marry his niece the next. Looks bad." Sir Parr Stitt pulled at his beard thoughtfully. "After we've drawn up the marriage settlement, I'll withdraw my forces and go home for a while. Wait for the gossip to blow over."

So between them, the two old people bent the law into a comfortable shape.

There was no trial the following day. The sheriff's bailiff stopped looking important, unlocked the door of the gatehouse chamber and let Sir Taxe go free. The released prisoner skulked round the castle, a ghost of his former self, and kept to the shadows.

Having arranged the family affairs to her entire satisfaction, Lady Crippling smoothed everything over by a lavish show of hospitality. She gave presents all round, congratulated Sir Bastion and Sir Tenley on the way they had rescued Myste, then ordered the sheriff's kitchen staff to prepare a feast. This was not easy at such short notice. They didn't exactly raid the larder, they raided Great Sterlyng village instead.

As Sir Tiff Fide became anxious and agitated the moment Myste left his sight, Sir Bastion had to visit the invalid in order to talk to her. They would have spent a long happy morning all three together, if Sir Tiff Fide's mind had not invented so many war-like heroes for her to marry. The only times he stopped describing them was when his wheezy lungs ran out of breath. Sir Bastion and Myste looked at each other and realized that their situation was more hopeless than ever.

The food was ready by late afternoon and the cheerful notes of a horn summoned the company to the feast.

Hurrying footsteps echoed through the castle, converging on the hall. Sir Parr Stitt came eagerly, shuffling through the great door, followed by Sir Prize, equally keen but with more dignity. Sir Bastion, Sir Tenley, and Sir Cum Stance arrived next. Father Off and Lady Ida Dora entered the room supporting Lady Super between them. She still wept like a fountain, but dried her eyes often enough to shoot angry glances at Sir Taxe, who had crept noiselessly into a dark corner. He had only come because he was hungry.

At long last, the door at the dais end of the hall opened

and old Lady Crippling came hobbling in with Myste stepping lightly behind her, like spring following winter. Sir Tiff Fide had finally given her permission to leave him and attend the feast. She looked wonderfully pretty in a gown of brocaded silk trimmed with ermine and fastened with little gold buttons. The overgown had a jewelled band of gold running all the way down the middle and long hanging sleeves. Lady Super recognized these splendid garments with a shock: they came from her chest.

A serving boy stood waiting with a large silver bowl in one hand, a ewer in the other, and a towel thrown over his shoulder. He poured thyme-scented water over the outstretched hands of the guests and dried them with the towel.

After this, the important guests seated themselves at the high table, while the rest of the company jostled together on benches along the wall side of the trestle tables; then everyone looked expectantly at a large wooden screen that stood at the lower end of the hall. There were three archways behind it: the wine came from the buttery to the left; the bread from the pantry at the right; and the meat was carried all the way along a passage from the kitchen, through the middle archway and round the screen. A trumpet heralded its arrival and – having been tasted as a precaution against poison by the pantry lad – it was served with much pomp from the front of the tables.

There was no venison or boar's meat because no one had gone hunting; but swans had been hastily dragged from the moat and were triumphantly carried in, having been cooked and re-dressed in their feathers. There were plenty of other courses, for Great Sterlyng village had supplied a strange mixture of food: capons, ducks, geese, hares, rabbits, herons, cormorants, pikes, sturgeons, carp and eels. The swans were carved into chunks and the pieces were served at the knife's end, to be picked off

daintily with the fingers; but some of the other meats had
been so heavily disguised, so pounded, pulped, seasoned
and spiced, that it was difficult to tell what beast, fish, or
bird they originally came from. Some courses were eaten
with a knife and the fingers; while others needed a spoon
and the fingers. Every so often the guests laid down their
knives and spoons and wiped their hands on the edge of
the tablecloth, for it was greasy work.

As usual at a feast, each couple shared a drinking cup, and Myste was miserable because she did not share hers with Sir Bastion. He had been seated far away at one of the side tables. She shared it with Sir Parr Stitt. The old man sucked his wine through his beard and gobbled his food as if he couldn't shovel it down fast enough. From time to time he stopped and peered at Myste, trying to get her face into focus and a rough idea of what she looked like.

Sir Bastion sighed as he gazed at Myste. She looked like a princess in those splendid clothes and – like a princess – she had become isolated and remote. Even her character had changed: her movements were stiff and proud; not shy as they used to be.

Lady Crippling was wishing she wasn't sharing her wine cup with Sir Prize. Every time she took it up, it seemed to be empty.

Sir Prize glowed pleasantly as the wine went down and found that his original horror of Lady Crippling was beginning to fade. He almost admired her. Strong-willed, he decided, puffed up and domineering; but – taken all in all – a splendid creature.

"I drink to your very good health," he cried for the third time, taking a long swig at the Burgundy.

Lady Crippling did not acknowledge the toast. She had finished calculating the probable terms of the marriage settlement between Sir Parr Stitt and Myste; but now she remembered her other problem – Sir Pressitt. Who would lead the army against him, now that Sir Taxe was behaving in such a spineless manner?

Sir Prize was pointing his knife at Myste and speaking with his mouth full. "Fine looking girl. Ought to be married. My son Bastion needs a wife – told me so the other day." He had altered his opinion, now that she was an heiress.

The food and drink was having a good effect on Lady

Crippling as well. She felt wonderfully sharp witted and resourceful. It suddenly occurred to her that she might be able to use the old fool at her side. She stole a sly glance at Sir Parr Stitt, who had eaten too much too quickly, and had fallen asleep, slumped forward on the table. She picked up the cup, found it empty, laid it heavily on the cloth and lowered her voice.

"The lady Myste needs a strong hard-hitting knight to defend her rights."

"Bastion had the strength to knock Sir Charge off his horse," boasted Sir Prize, at the same time trying to dislodge a tough piece of heron that had got stuck between his teeth.

"She also requires a man of wealth. I doubt if your son has much of a yearly income."

"He doesn't have any," said Sir Prize with sudden honesty, picking up the side of the tablecloth and using it to wipe his beard. His admiration for Lady Crippling was beginning to fade, but he didn't give up. "My wide demesne will come to the boy after my death. The lands of Sterlyng Castle and Chasemwell Hall lie side by side. Join 'em together and they make the largest single holding in the country – sheriff excepted."

There was a loud snort from Sir Parr Stitt as he slipped

from his chair and slid under the table. He was picked up by two squires and carried off to bed. Lady Crippling helped herself to some sugar plums and watched him go and then turned to Sir Bastion as he sat staring glumly at Myste. He had certainly done well in his fight against Sir Charge, so why not use him in the assault on Sir Pressitt? Sir Prize as well, for that matter. She did not hesitate to put this plan into action, using much craft and flattery.

"Sir Bastion's a stout-hearted warrior, but hardly in the same class as yourself. I remember the way you defeated my son, Sir Taxe. Your skill was magnificent!"

"I was rather good," admitted Sir Prize. "It comes with practice."

"That villain Sir Pressitt has foully wronged me. He raided my castle, rough-handled me as if I was no better than a serving wench, tied me up, gagged me and bound me to a faldstool. I want my revenge. Sir Taxe has lost all stomach for war. He lacks fire and determination . . ."

"And courage," suggested Sir Prize.

"He hasn't had your training and experience . . ."

"Gives up too easily."

Lady Crippling was fast losing her temper. "Now if you and your son would join forces with Sir Taxe against Sir Pressitt . . ."

Sir Prize conjured up a blurred vision of himself leading an army into battle and the wine made it attractive. What a splendid idea! He waggled a greasy finger under Lady Crippling's nose and issued his ultimatum: "I'll fight against Sir Pressitt on condition that Bastion can have the lady Myste to wife. With her he'll have – in due course – the castle, outlying manors, mills, holdings, sheep-farms, corn-lands, meadow-lands, pastures . . ."

The dream was rudely interrupted by Lady Crippling banging on the table, loudly calling for silence. Her mind, working faster than ever, had just produced a magnificent new idea; a way of recruiting even more knights to her cause. It would be the best piece of double-dealing of her life – a real master plan. Calling for her wine cup to be filled right up to the brim, Lady Crippling flourished it in the air and declared that she would give the hand of the maid Myste Tiff Fide to whichever knight proved himself worthy of her in the war against Sir Pressitt.

Sir Prize listened with his mouth open; then opened it much wider to complain loudly that this wasn't what he had intended, but his voice was drowned in the general tumult of cheering. Myste stared at her great-grandmother in utter bewilderment, then felt wonderfully reassured as she looked down the table and saw the gleaming eyes of Sir Bastion. At last, they had been given a chance.

Lady Crippling woke up next morning with a terrible hangover, absolutely appalled at what she had done. What could she say to Sir Prize and all the other knights, once Castle Skint had been successfully taken? How could Myste marry any one of them when she had already been promised to Sir Parr Stitt? Her headache worsened as she tried to scheme a way out, and she was really quite ill before she came across the solution. It was simple: once the fighting was over and she had no further need of them, she would commend the knights for bravery and declare they had all fought wonderfully well – but equally well. As Myste could not marry them all, it would be better for them to receive something else instead. Lady Crippling decided she could afford to be generous – she would hand out splendid gifts – and everyone would go home satisfied.

Sir Parr Stitt, she remembered, had told her to keep the marriage plan a strict secret; so she kept it secret. Even Myste knew nothing about it.

Sir Prize and Sir Taxe rode side by side along the forest track leading back to Castle Skint. They didn't talk much. Now that Sir Taxe was out of the clutches of the sheriff's bailiff and away from the scornful eyes of his wife, he had recovered some of his spirits; but he took every remark made by Sir Prize as a veiled insult, whereas Sir Prize was intolerably puffed-up and overbearing. Sir Bastion, Sir Tenley and Sir Cum Stance chatted as they trotted merrily after, while all Sir Prize's armed men straggled along behind.

They found Sir Charge standing shamefacedly in the middle of the deserted camp, almost alone except for Hugo First and a few loyal men. Sir Taxe's huge army had refused to obey him: some soldiers had deserted and gone home, while others had simply taken their weapons and gone wildly rampaging through the nearby villages, completely out of hand; looting everything in sight and setting fire to the peasants' huts. The carpenters hadn't done a stroke of work, leaving the giant trebuchet standing gaunt against the sky, abandoned and unfinished.

Sir Pressitt and his men had snatched their opportunity by making sudden raids; swooping out of a little side postern, charging through the camp and carrying off valuable supplies of food and arrows. Anyone venturing within range of their cross-bows was likely to be shot and their catapult continued to hurl stones at regular intervals.

As soon as the news got round to Sir Taxe's men that Sir Prize was marching his army into their camp, they grabbed their weapons and loot, left the outlying villages, and hurried back to defend it. They didn't want their tents and shelters to be taken over by anyone else. There was a terrible uproar when the two armies met; endless fights and bloody scrimmages.

It took a long time to restore law and order. Sir Bastion and Sir Tenley felt quite battle-weary at the end of the day, as they walked over the muddy tufts of grass towards Sir Taxe's pavilion, where the joint commanders were going to hold a formal council of war.

"It's a strange turn of events when you have to batter down the walls of a neighbour's castle in order to marry the girl of your choice," remarked Sir Bastion, always ready to talk about Myste.

"It's worth fighting for – inheriting Sterlyng Castle, I mean," said Sir Tenley teasingly. "I'm going to do the best I can."

"I'm going to marry Myste, and I'd sooner be dead than let another man win her," cried Sir Bastion, glaring angrily back.

Inside the pavilion, they found Sir Taxe and Sir Prize seated opposite each other on identical faldstools of gilded wood. Every suggestion made by the one was immediately vetoed by the other.

Sir Prize had managed to convince himself that he knew all there was to know about warfare. Wearing his old faded surcoat, he carried his battered flat-topped helm under his arm wherever he went and looked as if he'd been born in a tent and spent the whole of his life fighting.

172

This grizzled warrior started off by suggesting that one of the towers should be undermined. But Sir Taxe quickly replied that anyone with eyes in his head could see that Castle Skint was built on rock and the task was impossible.

"In which case we must build a siege tower and advance over the wall." Sir Prize spoke ponderously, rather too loudly.

"Only a fool would waste his strength climbing up to the top of a siege tower when he can breach the wall with a battering ram and walk through it," countered Sir Taxe.

Sir Charge was sitting uncomfortably on the straw palliasse, squashed between Sir Tenley – whom he despised – and Sir Bastion – whom he could not forgive for having defeated him. It was his turn to make a suggestion. "The gonne arrived yesterday from the iron foundry," he said, "we could use that against the enemy."

Sir Prize gave a loud snort of disgust. "New-fangled nonsense!" He'd never seen a cannon, but he had a strong prejudice against them.

Sir Taxe, on the other hand, had forgotten he had ordered

the weapon and was jubilant. "Our troubles are over!" he rejoiced. "The castle's as good as taken. We have only to fire the gonne and the walls will crumble like plaster."

"Fool's invention, gunpowder. Only good for fireworks," Sir Prize continued without listening. "It'll never be used in serious warfare. That gonne couldn't batter down the walls of a hen house – not if it was set down beside one."

"I beg to differ," cried Sir Charge, who had a proprietary interest in the cannon, having suggested it. "It's the weapon of the future. In fifty years' time, our traditional war machines – catapults, ballistas, trebuchets and the like – will be completely out of date."

"Rubbish. It's nothing but a great noise."

Sir Taxe was about to say something when he started listening instead. There was a strange whistling sound. The next second both he and Sir Prize fell from their faldstools and flattened themselves on the carpet. "Whizz. Zing." A long object shot through the roof of the pavilion – in one side and out the other – leaving two gaping holes edged with shreds of fluttering silk brocade.

Sir Tenley crawled out from under the camp bed, where he had hidden himself, hurried outside and came back with a giant arrow in his hand. The shaft was about six feet long and was made of wood covered with metal. There was an iron head and the tail was feathered with brass.

"It's a bolt from a ballista," said Sir Charge, who knew about these things. "They must have mounted the machine on a platform inside the curtain wall and fired it through one of the gaps in the parapet."

Sir Taxe rose from his knees and went outside to shake his fist at Sir Pressitt who was strutting up and down the hoarding at the top of the keep. He was proud as a turkey cock about the ballista. Old Hammer had found the ancient machine among the bits of rubbish in the smithy and Hugh Woods had helped to repair it. It looked like a giant cross-

bow and worked the same way. When he saw the angry figure of Sir Taxe, Sir Pressitt waved gleefully back.

Sir Taxe stalked back to his pavilion. "We'll use the gonne at once," he declared.

The cannon was hauled over the grass to a position on the south side of the castle. It was securely lashed to a wooden stand, while a brazier was placed nearby, with a charcoal fire burning in it.

Sir Pressitt's grin left his face and he started chewing one side of his moustache. He didn't know what to expect from a cannon, but he feared the worst. His men were equally anxious as they prepared to defend themselves against a sudden breach in the wall.

A young lad from the iron foundry stood by the cannon, waiting to fire it. At a signal from Sir Taxe, he took a handful of gunpowder out of a waxed canvas bag, put it on a ladle, shoved it into the powder chamber, and then rammed it down with a bundle of rags tied to the end of a long stick. The round stone ball was placed on top.

Everyone held their breath as the heated rod was taken out of the fire and bravely placed in the touch hole.

BANG!!!

The noise was terrific. Sir Pressitt nearly fell through one of the gaps in the wooden hoarding and all the horses in the camp – including Passemall – pulled up the pegs that tethered them, stampeded with fright, and charged wildly through the tents before disappearing into the forest. The wooden stand collapsed and the stone ball lifted itself heavily from the mouth of the cannon, lurched a few feet into the air, bounced twice on the ground and then dribbled slowly down the slope of the ditch and came to rest at the bottom. It did not even touch the wall.

The garrison inside the castle went mad with joy. "Do it again!" yelled Sir Pressitt, waving his immense sword in the air.

"Told you it was a damn-fool weapon," muttered Sir Prize.

Sir Charge was very red in the face. He tucked his chin in, stuck out his chest, marched up to the cannon and thrust the boy aside. He had huge hands, and he filled them with powder from the bag, heaped it on to the ladle, and rammed it down into the powder chamber until it was solid. There was only just enough room to put the second ball on top.

"Does firing a gonne qualify as a deed of valour?" Sir Bastion whispered to Sir Tenley. He looked worried as he watched Sir Charge heat up the rod. It would be unthinkable for him to win Myste.

Sir Charge marched the three paces back to the cannon and thrust the red-hot iron into the touch hole.

"This time it will be more effective," said Sir Taxe confidently.

It was. After a short pause, when everyone crowded round to see what was wrong, the cannon exploded in every direction but the right one. The stone ball stayed more or less where it was, and mixed splinters of wood and wrought iron shot haphazardly this way and that through the crowd. The casualties were appalling.

Sir Pressitt regarded the incident of the cannon as a great victory for himself. There were wild celebrations inside Castle Skint that night.

"Leave them to their own devices and they'll destroy their entire armies," he boasted, drinking toast after toast to his enemies.

More than three weeks had passed and Sir Taxe and Sir Prize were still laying siege to Sir Pressitt. It was getting cold, camping outside Castle Skint and the men inside were running out of food; but the armies worked with greater efficiency than before. All parties had got into the swing of it, so to speak.

Viewed from a distance, the castle looked as if it was being used for a gigantic game of pitch and toss. Sir Pressitt's men loaded their catapult with huge stones torn from the tumble-down buildings of his bailey and hurled them at the enemy camp. As catapults were mounted in a fixed position, unable to swivel, they landed on a strip of land the besieging army had learnt to avoid. Sir Taxe's men quickly fetched the blocks, loaded them on their own machines – now working – and hurled them back again.

Regularly each morning all the castle refuse was put in a sack which the catapult tossed over the wall in the hopes of spreading disease among the enemy. It was also a good way of getting rid of the rubbish.

The giant trebuchet was the most impressive war machine of them all. It towered above the men working it and made them look like ants. The arm was about fifty feet long with a net hanging at the end of it, and the counterweight of stone and sand was estimated to be as heavy as ten Flemish stallions, all standing together.

"Old-fashioned war machines are the best," Sir Prize remarked for the hundredth time as he watched the great arm being winched down. The men puffed and panted as

they rolled a huge corner stone into the net.

"It's safer than a gonne," said Sir Bastion, hurrying past. Then he stopped to watch Hugo First release the catch with a blow from a mallet. The great weight dropped down, bringing the arm up with an easy sweep. The stone left the net, disappeared into a low cloud, reappeared and came crashing down on the roof of the keep, hidden behind the parapet.

"It's remarkably accurate," said Sir Bastion.

"They'll never find anything to better it." Blissfully happy, Sir Prize was prepared to spend all day watching it, but Sir Bastion left, saying he was sorry he couldn't wait, he was needed back at his post.

As the joint commanders never agreed about anything, and as Sir Charge and Sir Cum Stance quarrelled almost as badly, no one seemed to notice that the real work of organizing the army had been left to Sir Bastion. He saw to it that each knight took a company of men and set them to work as far away from the other knights as possible. It was an excellent arrangement.

Sir Cum Stance found himself instructing the carpenters on how to build a siege tower. It was almost ready: three storeys high, with ladders leading from one floor to the next and a drawbridge at the top, the estimated height of the curtain wall. The rickety structure was mounted on wheels so that it could be pushed down the slope to the wall.

Sir Charge – still bruised and bandaged after the affair of the cannon – was commanding the battering ram. The carpenters had made something like a long shed on wheels and a beam about eighty feet long was slung from the roof of it. A splendid iron ram's head was fitted to the end of this beam; an animal with a sharp nose, like a beak.

"It's a good omen," Sir Taxe told everyone with grim satisfaction, pointing from the ram's head to the gold ram painted on his shield. He felt in a good mood for shouting abuse at Sir Pressitt, but when he looked up at the top of the keep he noticed with disappointment that he wasn't there. Sir Taxe had not seen him for several days, and wondered if he was ill.

When he wasn't inspecting the battering ram, Sir Taxe was sitting in his pavilion dictating glowing accounts of how the siege was progressing to a scrivener. Lady Crippling expected a letter almost every day, and the messengers were tired of galloping back and forth through the forest. They knew every tree.

To get the siege tower and battering ram up against the wall, it was necessary for the ditch to be filled in at two places. This was dangerous work for the men, and the only person who was happy to command them was Sir Tenley. He said it gave him a chance to prove his valour. He seemed to lead a charmed life as he walked about through showers of arrows, directing his mud-covered serfs as they shovelled stones and rubble into the ditch, filling in odd corners with straw and earth, packing it down by stamping on it, and finishing the job with a neat surface of halved tree trunks.

The enemy did all they could to harass the work and keep their ditch as a ditch. Leaning over the wall, they dropped down anything they could lay hands on: stones, iron bars, pots of quick lime, more stones, burning pitch, a cauldron or two of boiling water, stones again, and an odd assortment of rusty kitchen pans.

Sir Tenley's men adored him; they would peer out from the safety of their rough shelters of wood covered with animal hides and gasp as they saw a huge boulder being toppled over the parapet just above his unprotected head. Sir Tenley's movements were jerky and unpredictable. He would stop and pull out an arrow that had got lodged between the joints of his armour just as the boulder thumped down on the very spot where he should have been standing. He was hit only once. That was when Willy Doolittle got hold of an old wooden bucket that had once been used for the well and, creeping to the edge of the wall, dropped it with such accurate aim that it landed upside down on Sir Tenley's head. For once Sir Tenley was really frightened: he could not make out what had happened. Waving his arms like a windmill, he stumbled to the side of the ramp and was about to fall over the edge into the ditch when a soldier grabbed his gauntlet and led him to safety. The bucket was completely jammed on to his helm, and had to be prized off by one of the smiths.

Sir Bastion did what he could to preserve his friend's life. Arrows from his archers whistled over the heads of the serfs working in the ditch, aimed at any of Sir Pressitt's men who dared to show themselves on the battlements.

Things were going badly inside the castle and Sir Pressitt had realized, with increasing despondency, that the tide of war had turned against him. He had stopped strutting along the hoardings – as noticed by Sir Taxe – he had stopped strutting anywhere; he sat in his hall and was careful not to look out of the windows. After a while he developed the habit of staying in bed, declaring there was no point in taking a rich prize if you didn't make full use of it.

Each morning Sir Pressitt woke from his slumbers and bellowed for Willy Doolittle to bring his morning drink and portion of bread. Then he would pull his shirt out from under his pillow, put it on, and spend the rest of the day leaning back against the splendid headboard, looking at the carved canopy above him. He tried to ignore the great stones as they came crashing through the roof, landing with an almighty thump on the floor above. When it rained, the water flooded the upper storey, seeped through cracks between the boards and dripped the full thirty feet into buckets and pans laid out on the rushes to catch it.

One day it was Ivor Grudge who answered the breakfast summons, carrying nothing.

"Where's my bread?" demanded Sir Pressitt, pulling the sheet round his neck to keep out the cold, while his thin hair stood up round his head like a spiky halo.

"There b'aint none," growled Grudge.

"Why? Didn't they bake any?"

"No. On account o' there being no flour."

"Oatmeal biscuits?" inquired Sir Pressitt hopefully. "Or what about a chicken?"

"You ate the last bird, dinner time yesterday."

"So. We'll have to start on the pigeons under the roof."

"See here my lord, they've got us beat," cried Grudge urgently. "We've none of us had a bite to eat and that's not the worst on it. If you hearken well, you'll hear how they're a-battering our wall with a ram."

Sir Pressitt hearkened and heard a dull thumping sound. He hurriedly felt under the pillow, pulled out his shirt, and put it on inside out. "I'll get up and arm myself," he cried in a sudden panic.

In next to no time, Sir Pressitt was again standing on the hoarding at the top of his keep. When he looked down, he saw with a pang of horror that everything was ready for the planned assault. The stoutly-built siege tower stood poised at the edge of the forest, waiting to be filled with armed men and pushed down the hill. The shed carrying the battering ram was standing on the ramp nearest the gatehouse, and the whole structure had been wedged firmly into place. The roof of raw hides plastered down with clay hid the men working it, but Sir Pressitt could well imagine them swinging the beam backwards and forward. He could hear their lusty singing and the sharp beat of iron smiting stone.

"By Lucifer! They'll be through the wall and into the bailey by tomorrow!" exclaimed Sir Pressitt. Then he caught sight of Sir Taxe and quickly went down to spend the rest of the day in his hall. He didn't feel like exchanging insults: not in the present situation.

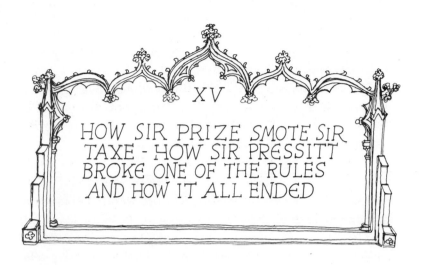

XV

HOW SIR PRIZE SMOTE SIR TAXE - HOW SIR PRESSITT BROKE ONE OF THE RULES AND HOW IT ALL ENDED

Sir Pressitt did not sleep a wink all that night. As soon as it was light, he got out of bed, climbed the stairs to the gallery running round the top of his hall and looked out of one of the large arched windows. The weather was cold and damp, but it wasn't actually raining. Soon, he heard the rough voices of his men and the steady thump of the battering ram. He went back to bed in a panic, to warm himself up and decidé what to do about it.

After a while, footsteps came clattering up the stairs and Ivor Grudge and Hugh Woods rushed wildly in.

"What do you want?" cried Sir Pressitt, sitting up in his shirt.

"We've come for your feather mattress," they declared. "It's needed for the defence of the wall."

"Have you gone mad?" screamed Sir Pressitt. "You can't fight with feathers!"

Grudge hastily explained that they had spent the previous day lowering palliasses down the wall to cushion it against the battering ram and now they had run out of palliasses.

"There's nothing left, but your mattress."

Sir Pressitt flung his arms round the huge, feather-filled

183

bag and gripped it tightly. "Never. It's part of the prize. To use it would be to admit defeat."

The servants were in a rebellious mood. There was a disgraceful scuffle. The two burly men took the mattress by the corners, pulled it up and tipped Sir Pressitt on the rush covered floor. Then they hurried it away.

Outside the castle, Sir Prize was leading his army away from the camp towards the siege tower which had been pushed out of the shelter of the trees and stood at a distance just out of bow-shot of the castle wall. Behind, marched Sir Bastion, Sir Tenley and Sir Cum Stance. The column entered the tower, and soon every inch of floor space was occupied by heavily-armed men.

Sir Taxe stood sword in hand before his assembled army, watching the battering ram pound the remains of the last palliasse to shreds of sackcloth and chaff. The gold ram embroidered on his jupon heaved with excitement as he waited to see the little patch of daylight that would show they had tunnelled right through the wall.

High up on the gatehouse, Willy Doolittle loaded the catapult with a sack of all the refuse he had been able to find in the kitchen, and – as a final gesture of defiance – launched it at the enemy. It landed neatly at Sir Taxe's feet, spilling out over the ground and spattering his newly-burnished greaves. Giving it a scornful glance, he stepped back a pace.

"A blow from Sir Taxe's ram!" loudly chorused the men, swinging the beam against the wall with a resounding smack. The stones under the wreck of the palliasse splintered and crumbled.

Sir Taxe smiled as he watched, then opened his eyes wide and stood frozen with horror: he saw his own feather mattress creeping down the grey wall, dangling ignominiously at the end of two ropes. It dropped into place just as the battering ram drew back for the next hard stroke.

"Stop!" yelled Sir Taxe.

His voice was drowned by the noisy singing. He stepped forward, slipped on a pigeon skin and fell flat on his face in the mud.

"A blow from Sir Taxe's ram!"

The great beam thrust forward and buried its iron beak-like nose in the very centre of the fat mattress. The huge bag burst with a bang. A dense cloud of feathers, like a miniature snowstorm, rose slowly into the air and drifted this way and that; swirling, floating and hovering. They settled on swords, stuck to bowstrings, whirled and eddied round sharp blades of spears, axes and halberds, got inside helms and crept up visors.

The next blow from the battering ram breached the wall and the miners, coughing, sneezing and cursing the feathers, quickly cleared the loose stones and widened the breach.

Muddy, furious and on his feet again, Sir Taxe plunged through the dark ragged hole. He was so enraged at the destruction of his mattress that he forgot to be frightened and went into the attack bellowing like a bull. Sir Charge followed him at the head of a picked company of men, while Hugo First stayed behind in command of the rear guard.

As Sir Taxe and his army poured into the bailey, Sir Pressitt's men gave them one terrified look, turned and bolted for the keep faster than they had ever bolted before. They rushed up the entrance steps just as Sir Pressitt – fully armed – was coming down. They swept him backwards into the little guard tower and Hugh Woods, with the speed of a monkey, climbed up to the room above and let the portcullis fall with a crash. After this, they all fled to the forebuilding, pulled up the drawbridge, lowered the second portcullis and then barred and bolted the huge main door of the keep.

"Hang me!" panted Grudge. "I thought we was done for."

"We're safe enough in here," said Sir Pressitt, peering through one of the narrow windows and then crossing over to peer through the other. He could see Sir Taxe's army swarming all round the keep; yelling out threats and beating the stone with their weapons. "They'll never batter their way through these walls. Why, they must be over twelve feet thick at the base."

All this time, the siege tower had been swaying precari-
ously down the slope. It tottered on to the ramp that had
been made for it and came to rest against the wall with a
tremendous jolt. The drawbridge at the top was lowered to
the battlements and Sir Prize – to do him credit – was the
first to stride across.

"Advance for the honour of Chasemwell Vale. Sha hou,
sha hou, sha hou," he bellowed, flourishing his sword.

Sir Bastion hooted like a hunting horn and followed his
father.

"Hoo arere!" whooped Sir Tenley, with another cry of
the chase.

Sir Cum Stance joined in, followed by a wild chorus as
the soldiers leapt down from the wall to attack the enemy
they expected to find guarding the entrance to the keep.
Sir Taxe and his men, astonished by the noise, turned to
stare at them. Now Sir Taxe's jupon was well plastered
with a mixture of mud and feathers and he was quite
unrecognizable; while, to make matters worse, another

feather had somehow got stuck in the sight of Sir Prize's ancient flat-topped helm and he could hardly see at all.

"Yield, horrid varlet," hooted Sir Prize, delivering a crashing blow on the top of the iron hat; attacking with a savagery that would have done credit to a bear.

"He's out to murder me!" screamed Sir Taxe.

"Take that, you rascally villain," continued Sir Prize, pleased that he was getting the best of the fight.

Sir Bastion, suddenly understood what had happened and came between them. "Put up your sword, father," he said.

"Out of my way – vermin."

In desperation, Sir Bastion threw down his own weapon and grabbed his father's sword arm with both hands. There was a fierce struggle, for Sir Prize's blood was up and he was in a good fighting mood. It took some time to convince the old man of his mistake.

"Eh? What?" came his confused voice from inside the helm. "Dithering idiot. What did he want to attack me for?"

After this, all the soldiers rested on their weapons and stared glumly at the great thick walls of the keep; a second hard nut to crack.

It was evening. Sir Pressitt slowly climbed the winding stairway leading to his hall in the keep, feeling very tired. His men were in a state of revolt. They were hungry and there wasn't a scrap of food to eat; everyone had gone to bed without supper.

Sir Pressitt was longing to sink down into the soft feather mattress; but when he looked into the great bedstead, there were only the leather thongs and cords stretched across the bottom of the frame. Wearily, he gathered up an armful of rushes from the floor and stuffed them into the empty space. It looked like the nest of some huge bird. Throwing sheets over the rushes, he covered them with the blankets and laid the brocaded silk coverlet on top. Then he took off his shirt, braies and hose, left them lying on the floor and crept into bed, wrapping himself round in one of the sheets.

He was about to fall asleep when he remembered he had hidden a leather bottle of wine under the bedstead. He couldn't find it in the dark as he groped among the rushes with his hand, so he got out of bed and, walking softly among his sleeping men, went to a chest at the far side of the room where a lamp burned all night.

This lamp was a makeshift affair: just an earthenware bowl filled with fish oil with a wick of twisted cord floating in it. The flame gave off a thick black smoke, but it helped Sir Pressitt to find what he was searching for. Climbing back to bed, he laid the lamp carelessly on the silk coverlet and drank until the bottle was empty. Then he rolled on to his side, sighed deeply and went to sleep.

Turning over upset the lamp. Smelly oil soaked into the fine brocade and dripped on to the wool blankets below. Sir Pressitt slept soundly while the flame from the wick ran along the silk, danced brightly over him and then descended to the dirty rushes, which caught fire at once, thus setting light to the bed posts.

Sir Pressitt was dreaming about the day of judgement: his soul had been put on the scales, his sins weighed against him and Saint Michael the Archangel had cast him into Hell. It was hotter than he had expected. When he awoke, the flames were still there. Sir Pressitt leapt out of the bonfire shouting like a soul in torment. He quickly scrambled into his shirt and braies, still yelling loudly for help.

The men all sleeping on the rushes at the other side of the arcade, woke up, rubbed their eyes and stared at the burning bedstead. Pointing at the well shaft in the centre of the room, Sir Pressitt ordered them to pour water over it, but they refused to obey. The room was a good thirty feet high and the flames were leaping up and licking the broken timbers of the floor above. It smelt like a good log fire until the blankets caught properly, after which the stench was terrible.

"Damn fellah's set fire to his keep," observed Sir Prize, standing outside his pavilion, looking at the bright light that had woken him, shining through the round-headed windows. He had flung a fur-lined cloak over his shirt and was stamping about on the cold wet grass in his bare feet.

"I wonder what could have happened," said Sir Bastion, wrapped in a blanket.

"We'll find out soon enough in the morning," was the reply as his father stumped back to bed.

The light in the great square building stopped glowing like a Hallowe'en lamp; it flickered, faded and disappeared.

Next morning Sir Pressitt called for a parley. He walked across the bailey under a flag of truce, disappeared inside one of the mural towers, and climbed out on the roof. He looked even more ferocious than usual: fully armed, his face black with soot, and half his moustache burned off. He stared down at Sir Taxe and Sir Prize who stood waiting, surrounded by their knights, squires, and the multitude of men-at-arms, archers, miners, carpenters, household servants and boys. He felt like an actor on a stage about to perform a bloody tragedy. He was just about to launch into his opening lines when his eye was suddenly attracted by a glittering cavalcade trotting through the dark trees of the forest: a horse litter, three ladies mounted on fine palfreys, an old knight riding a sturdy charger, a priest kicking along a mule, and a whole retinue of servants. It was Lady Crippling coming to enjoy her revenge. Sir Pressitt's eye passed quickly over the figures of Myste, Lady Super and Lady Ida Dora; but became transfixed and utterly hypnotized by the sight of the man on the charger. Although he was fatter and quite a different colour – Sir Pressitt still recognized the ragged ghost he had met in the forest. Sir Tiff Fide! It gave him a terrible shock. Had the whole world turned against him, that even this old man must rise up from his prison grave to reproach him? Sir Pressitt hastily averted his eyes and saw a solitary knight approaching on a tall black horse. Another bad omen. Sir Pressitt wondered if it was the Devil himself.

191

If it was the Devil, then he was in league with the enemy, for when the horseman arrived he was greeted like a long-lost friend by Sir Prize and his son Sir Bastion. Then the cavalcade from Sterlyng Castle trotted into the camp and there were more cries of rejoicing and noisy reunions.

"Why, here's Sir Lute!" The happy voice of Myste rang through the air, clear as a bell.

"I've brought some interesting news," the lower tones of Sir Lute greeted his friends.

No actor likes his audience to turn its back on him, especially when he's playing a tragedy. "It's time for the parley, by Lucifer," interrupted Sir Pressitt, yelling from the top of the tower.

"Give us your news," said Sir Bastion.

"I'll keep it for later," replied Sir Lute. "It's of no real importance."

Down on the ground at the far side of the ditch, Sir Taxe and Sir Prize stood side by side in the expectant audience, tilting their heads up to look at Sir Pressitt. He was a tall man and he looked even taller standing on the top of a tower. Sir Taxe, who was small, felt at a disadvantage. He wanted to be higher up.

After a hurried consultation with Sir Prize, Sir Taxe informed his enemy that they would parley on equal levels. Accordingly the joint commanders marched across to the siege tower still standing on its hastily-made foundations. There was an unfortunate squabble as to who should proceed who up the stairs; but Sir Taxe was quicker on his feet and got there before Sir Prize. Standing on the highest storey, the two knights could be seen by everyone and were able to look down on Sir Pressitt in the most satisfactory manner.

"You surrender?" they cried in unison.

Sir Pressitt forgot his speech and made no reply. He just hauled a large sack over to the edge of the battlement, turned it upside down and emptied some grey-looking rubbish into the ditch.

"What is it?" asked Sir Taxe, peering over the edge of the siege tower.

"Can't make it out at all . . . damn fellah . . . looks like a load of wood ash."

"It's the relics of your bedstead," roared out Sir Pressitt. "Lie on that if you can." He pointed down to the ditch.

Striding over the wooden boards, Sir Prize leaned beside Sir Taxe to have a closer look. It was only a slight movement, but the green timbers gave an ominous creak, followed by another creak. Several stones in the mixture of wood, straw and rubble filling the ditch below, rumbled into different places, resulting in a sudden jerk to the structure above. The joint commanders clutched each other as – with slow deliberation – the siege tower toppled over and gently leant itself against a corner of the wall. The two knights, locked in an iron embrace, slid down the steeply sloping floor, dropped a short distance still clutching each other, and then fell apart as they crashed down on top of Sir Pressitt – knocking him sideways.

Sir Pressitt struggled to his feet and when he was sure of his balance, he launched himself at Sir Taxe, punched him a bit and then hugged him tightly, at the same time crying out to Ivor Grudge to do likewise with Sir Prize.

"Prisoners!" yelled Sir Pressitt, rejoicing in this sudden stroke of luck. "I hold them both prisoners. Hurry them to the keep and clap them in irons."

"No one can be taken prisoner in the middle of a parley!" exclaimed Sir Lute. "It's against the rules of warfare."

Sir Pressitt ignored this remark. He was busy shoving Sir Taxe in front of him down the narrow stairs of the tower.

Sir Bastion ran to his horse, vaulted into the saddle (no

193

mean feat, considering the weight of his armour) and drew his sword.

"Shame on me if I stand by and see my father taken," he cried, charging through the breach in the wall.

"I'll punish any false knight who breaks a parley," shouted Sir Lute, not waiting to mount his horse, but striding straightway into the bailey.

Sir Pressitt and his men were dragging their prisoners along towards the keep. Sir Taxe was twisting about and kicking, but Sir Prize had been knocked out by a hard blow on the helm. Grudge had him by the shoulders and Hugh Woods took his feet. They were trying to run with him swinging between them, a limp heavy weight.

Aiming to intercept them, Sir Bastion spurred straight for the entrance steps of the keep, but he was stopped by a solid wall of men who attacked him with spears, axes, war-hammers and halberds. They surged about him aiming fierce blows; several of them hanging on his foot, trying to pull him out of the saddle.

Seeing his friend hard beset, Sir Lute attacked the men attacking Sir Bastion. There were cries of anguish as they turned to encounter the sword that had fought in so many battles.

The tumult was doubled as some of Sir Pressitt's men screamed and ran for their lives. They were being chased by a savage animal – Passemall! He was kicking out with his hooves and biting with his teeth, while Sir Tenley hacked right and left with his sword; managing to stay in the saddle by some sort of lucky magic. Then Sir Charge and Sir Cum Stance came thundering into the arena, followed by a stream of foot soldiers, roaring out a mixture of battle cries and hunting calls, and the fighting became general.

"Get the prisoners inside!" Sir Pressitt's voice could still be heard above the tumult.

"Turn and defend yourself," roared Sir Charge, giving him a ponderous blow on the helm with a mace.

"Yield, black-hearted lying villain!" Sir Cum Stance smote him with a sword from the other side.

Sir Pressitt ducked, dropped Sir Taxe and sprinted clumsily across the bailey, cursing his heavy armour. He was aiming for one of the ruined buildings: the old hall, where his ancestors used to live. Behind it, there was a long secret passage leading down to the river. He turned, faced his enemies, and kept them at bay with wide swipes of his two-handed sword, stepping back as he did so. Soon he found himself stumbling over fallen stones and then took refuge behind the ancient stairway. One minute he

195

stood there, defiant and unyielding, and the next he had
ducked through a low ruined archway, half lost in the long
grass.

"Where can the villain have got to?" asked Sir Cum
Stance, dismounting and nervously exploring the ruin. He
regretted having clipped a visor to the brow of his helmet as
it restricted his vision.

"The earth seems to have swallowed him up," said Sir
Charge, who had also failed to notice Sir Pressitt's quick
action.

Meanwhile, Sir Lute had cut his way through the press
and reached Sir Bastion just as Sir Pressitt's men had pulled
him off his horse. Standing over him, holding the enemy
back with swift strokes of the sword, Sir Lute gave Sir
Bastion time to get to his feet again, then both together
they ran up the steps and stood shoulder to shoulder
before the door of the entrance tower to the keep.

Seeing their way barred, Grudge and Hugh Woods
dropped Sir Prize and gave themselves up.

After that, everyone laid down their weapons and enjoyed the spectacle of Passemall careering round and round the inside of the curtain wall, as if he was in a Roman circus. The excitement had driven him wild: he was out of control and running away as usual. Having finally tired of racing so hard and getting nowhere, he halted suddenly and Sir Tenley shot over his head in a neat somersault. He sat on the muddy ground and pointed his sword at Sir Bastion.

"There's no doubt which knight performed the bravest deed of arms," he said.

The armies roared their applause, for Sir Bastion was immensely popular.

Trumpets shrilled out as the drawbridge leading over the ditch was lowered, the portcullis raised, the great doors flung wide open and Lady Crippling entered the castle with great pomp; Myste and Sir Tiff Fide behind her, followed by Lady Super and Lady Ida Dora – Father Off between them – and a huge crowd. Everyone, in fact who had not taken part in the battle.

The old lady stumped along indomitably, her little black eyes darting here and there, eagerly searching for Sir Pressitt.

"Bring the villain before me," she cried. "I wish to see him grovelling in the dust, begging for mercy."

Sir Cum Stance and Sir Charge were walking sheepishly back from the ruin of the old hall, picking their way over the fallen stones.

"He's escaped somehow," Sir Charge admitted with a shake of the head. "Got clean away."

"Escaped? Gone? Am I not to see him humbled?" Lady Crippling looked dreadfully disappointed and rather pathetic: then she blazed into a fury. "Addle-headed fools. You've cheated me of my just revenge."

"We're not wanting in courage," said Sir Cum Stance

huffishly, "but those buildings are dangerous, dark and full of holes. I'm no knight for a rabbit burrow."

Hugo First was dispatched with a company of men to search the sheer rocky banks of the river: but they never found Sir Pressitt.

Meanwhile, Sir Bastion had gently unlaced his father's helm. Sir Prize sat up, threw back his mail coif and showed everyone a shiny bump on his bald head.

"I think my son's proved himself worthy of the maid Myste," he said in his best pompous manner.

The men-at-arms went wild with delight, clashing their weapons together and banging their fists on their shields.

Sir Tiff Fide came hobbling forward, fingering the edge of his new furred gown and opened his mouth to speak; but Lady Crippling impatiently pushed him back.

"Hold your noise and hear what I have to say," she cried before launching into her prepared speech: "Sirs. I thank you all heartily for coming to our aid against the villain Sir Pressitt." Loud cheers. "And now is the time to speak of the reward." More cheers. "It is my opinion that all these brave knights fought well . . ."

"Apart from Sir Cum Stance and Sir Charge, who let him escape," came a gruff voice from the crowd, followed by several groans.

". . . wonderfully well," repeated Lady Crippling, ignoring the interruption and ploughing on with her speech. "As they were all equally brave," she paused to let the point sink home, "I cannot decide who should claim the reward. Myste cannot marry them all . . ." It was no good. Her high-pitched rasping voice was drowned in a roar of protest. The lowest soldier knew that if Sir Bastion had not acted so quickly, Sir Taxe and Sir Prize would have been locked up inside the keep and Sir Pressitt could have demanded any terms he pleased for their release. Greatly embarrassed, Lady Crippling abandoned her plan altogether and had to resort to the truth.

"The situation has altered," she faltered, "Myste has recently and . . . er . . . unexpectedly received an offer of marriage from such an important person, she could hardly refuse without offending him. In short, she's going to be the wife of Sir Parr Stitt, your sherriff."

Myste listened to this blunt statement and then panicked. She forgot about being a fine lady and she forgot about the crowd. She simply fled to Sir Bastion and clung to him. It was a bit uncomfortable putting her arms round the neck of a man dressed entirely in iron, resting her head on his cloth-covered breastplate, but Myste didn't mind. She felt more secure there than anywhere else.

Sir Lute watched them both with a smile and then came striding over the muddy battlefield towards Lady Crippling.

"Lady, I have news for you," he said, frowning severely.

"It's all arranged," she blustered. "The marriage settlement has been drawn up and is waiting to be signed."

"I suggest you tear it up. Sir Parr Stitt is dead."

"It's all a lie . . . it's not true . . ."

"The court of the King's bench ruled – on my recommendation – that Sir Parr Stitt was too old to hold the office of sheriff. I was instructed to ride to his castle and inform him of the decision. I arrived too late. He's dead beyond a shadow of doubt."

"Murder. Treachery. Someone has poisoned him."

"Not at all. He died of over-eating."

For the first time in her long life, Lady Crippling found herself in such a tight corner, she could not think of a single crafty scheme to help her wriggle out of it. She looked across at Myste, still clinging to Sir Bastion, and her mind went blank.

Sir Tiff Fide stepped forward again, coughed and squared his shoulders. "I've always been an honourable knight," he said weezily, "kept faith . . . stuck to my word where I could. From now on, there will be no more double-dealings at Sterlyng Castle. And to prove it, my granddaughter Myste will be given to the man who has shown himself worthy of her in the field of battle – Sir Prize's son, Sir Bastion of Chasemwell Vale."